The Prince and the Snowgirl

The Prince and the Snowgirl

Simon Cheshire

PICCADILLY PRESS • LONDON

*This book is dedicated to anyone who correctly
decodes the references to a real-life person, which
are scattered inside this story.*

(And no, it's nobody royal. Or Edgar Allan Poe.)

First published in Great Britain in 2006
by Piccadilly Press Ltd.,
5 Castle Road, London NW1 8PR
www.piccadillypress.co.uk

A catalogue record for this book is available
from the British Library

ISBN: 1 85340 863 8
ISBN-13: 9 781853 408632

1 3 5 7 9 10 8 6 4 2

Printed and bound in Great Britain by Bookmarque Ltd
Cover design and text design and setting by Simon Davis
Cover illustration by Nicola Taylor

Set in 11.5 point Palatino

Chapter 1

This is the story of how everything changed, and of who I am. Or who I was. Or will be? It's not easy to say.

I'm changing, right now, as I look at myself. I'm sitting in a raised, black leather chair, in front of mirrors which run the whole length of the room, on the ground floor of a hotel in Scotland. I'm fifteen years old, I'm many miles from home, and upstairs, right now, in a messed-up bedroom, are the girl of my dreams and my best friend from school. My best friend is facing a serious crisis.

I am getting my hair cut.

'Are you sure you want so much off, sir?' says the young woman standing behind me. She's poised with the scissors above my head, as if they can't wait to get cutting and she's the only thing holding them back.

'Absolutely,' I say with a confidence I don't quite feel. 'I need a radical new look. It's got to be drastic.'

'OK,' she says quietly.

I spent the night, fully clothed, slumped in an armchair in that messed-up bedroom. I'm not at my freshest. I have an uncomfortable suspicion that the hairdresser can smell me.

I don't think she's been awake very long. Neither have I. It's still early in the morning. I had to tap on the glass door of this salon to attract her attention and get her to open the place up. I had to offer to pay extra, and with the prices they charge here that means I'm going to be stumping up an eye-watering amount of cash when this is over.

'Are you here on holiday?' she says.

'No,' I say, not wanting to be dragged into a conversation. She obviously hasn't twigged who I am.

No, who I WAS.

I think she's still gliding along on autopilot. In the mirror I can see an undrunk mug of steaming coffee sitting by the till. For the first time, I notice that her own hair is lank and stripy with overdone highlights. It doesn't exactly boost my confidence.

But there's no going back now. This is, as they say, the point of no return. Once this is done, I will have declared to the world that there's a NEW ME.

I came down here on a whim. The idea suddenly popped into my head and I ran all the way downstairs. I wanted to prove something to my friend, the one facing the crisis. I needed to make him see I was serious.

So I'm getting my hair cut.

As weird as it sounds, I'm changing the way I look to try

to help my friend. It's just coincidence that I also want to prove something to the girl of my dreams. And it's just coincidence that it's also marking a turning point in my life.

Or maybe it isn't coincidence at all. Maybe the last few days have been leading up to this.

I look at myself in the mirror. It's me, and it's not me. For such a long time now that face has been someone else too. Literally, someone else. For such a long time, I've had to be so fussy and careful about my hair, about my whole appearance. Not out of vanity, but because I've had to look a certain way.

Not any more. I'm determined. There's no going back.

The scissors close around the slightly curled, night-coloured mass that masks my forehead. A thick snip of hair tumbles to the floor, and my pulse dances unsteadily.

It's strange how you can look back in time at yourself and see someone so different. What makes it all the more strange is that I'm looking back on myself as I was just six weeks ago. That's all the time it takes for your life to have a complete makeover. Of course, some people's lives are changed in an instant, but those cases are usually something unforeseen, something they didn't plan or didn't see heading straight for them. An accident, or meeting someone.

This change, MY change, is voluntary. Completely. So it takes slightly longer. But even so, six weeks ago, I'd never have thought I'd be here now, sitting in this chair, looking at myself. Or what I think is me. Or what might be me, if I can decide who I really am.

Six weeks ago I was pretty sure of myself. I was convinced I'd got most things in my life fairly well sewn up. With one or two exceptions. Maybe I was even a little bit smug. Maybe I was just a little bit over-confident.

So. Six weeks ago . . .

'Oooh, he's not so tall in real life, is he?'

'Hellooo, Prince George! Prince George! . . . Look, poppet, that's the next king. What's that, poppet? No, darling, he's not a footballer.'

'Rubbish! Looks nuffin' like 'im!'

You see the sort of thing I have to contend with? I get that kind of stuff every time. Every time.

I smile sweetly. I know it's a sweet smile, because I've practised it so much in the bathroom mirror that I can do it without a second thought. It's a big, warm smile, sweet as a sugar cube dipped in chocolate. I can switch it on instantly, and it gets gooey grins in response from everyone I aim it at. Well, almost everyone.

'Nuffin' like 'im. 'E's rubbish!' mutters the big bloke in the woolly-collared coat.

Naturally, the big bloke's in a minority of one. The rest of the crowd are waving and shouting, jostling and holding up their digital cameras. There's a starscape of flashes twinkling all around me. Hands are held out to me, and I shake as many as I can, arms crossing and bending to get to everyone. I keep going with the smile. Works a treat.

It's a lovely feeling. Nothing quite like it. Being in front of a crowd of two or three hundred strangers, who all feel like they know you, and who are all pleased to see you (well, except the big bloke). It makes you feel so LIKED. Not loved, exactly, that's not quite it. Approved of, appreciated, endorsed . . . I dunno, you'd need a thesaurus to find the right word. It's very, very nice, anyway.

Even if it's all fake.

The manager of SuperSave nudges my elbow. 'Time to do the ribbon, sunshine.' He's a short, round man with a moustache like a yard broom. He glances at the crowd with a mixture of delight and surprise. Looks like I got me another happy client, yessirree!

I do pride myself on my accuracy. It takes a lot of practice, of course. A lot. And there's a surprising amount of research involved too – reading up on all the latest on the Prince George front, keeping up to date in terms of clothes and hair. You'd be surprised.

The hardest thing is body language. It's part of how you recognise someone. Everyone's got their own physical quirks and ways of moving. You don't normally take much conscious notice of it, but you know straight away when it's missing. I reckon it gives me a bit of an edge over the competition.

'Good crowd,' mutters the manager.

I wave to Joe Public, in exactly the right way, right arm slightly bent at the elbow, two short horizontal movements. I even do the little fingers-clipped-back-against-the-palm thing at the end, which nobody really sees this time except for me, but I think it's important to be, you know, complete. To stay in character, as actors say.

I'm ushered over to the main doors of the supermarket. A thick ribbon in the official SuperSave shade of blue is stretched across them. The manager hands me a big pair of scissors.

The crowd hushes. I take up position at the ribbon, with the scissors poised to cut.

Voice is another problem altogether. It can make a lot of difference to the overall effect. Some of the others on the agency's books simply can't get the voice AT ALL, and it's in their contracts that they don't speak a word. Others are better at the voice than anything else, quite frankly. Prince George's voice is actually slightly higher than mine, and I can't duplicate it without sounding just that little bit phoney. What I CAN do really well, though, is the accent, the cadence, the intonation. Posh, but not too RP, slightly sloping with some of the vowels.

'Good afternoon, everyone,' I say. 'Freezing cold January day, but at least the rain's kept away.' (This is adapted from an actual speech of Prince George's made a year ago at some horse and hounds thing. Always sounds a bit wet to me, but it's one hundred per cent authentic.)

'I'm delighted to be here to officially open the one hundred and second UK branch of SuperSave!'

A couple of small cheers from the crowd. The manager looks delighted again, this time mostly with himself.

Now the contractual obligation bit. 'As you know, ladies and gentlemen, SuperSave means super savings! Top quality and low, low prices! I must get my folks to come and buy stuff for the Palace garden parties here!'

Huge laugh! I threw the joke in for free. If the manager was any more chuffed he'd go pop.

'So, without further ado,' I say, 'I declare the Cubbington branch of SuperSave open!'

I snip the ribbon. Huge cheer! The doors slide aside, and the crowd shuffles along.

There's a few more minutes of me pressing the flesh with Joe Public. I sign some autographs. (In the lookalike business, you're supposed to sign your own name. It's a legal thing. But since the real Prince George isn't allowed to sign autographs at all, I don't see what the problem is. Still, I stick to the rule. Usually.)

The manager comes over and slaps me on the shoulder. 'Went well, sunshine!' Up close, his moustache looks like you'd turn up all kinds of fascinating information if you sent it to a forensics lab.

'Not bad at all,' I say.

Two very tall men stride out of nowhere and introduce themselves to the manager.

'Ed Goulding,' says the one in the spotless, dark blue

double-breasted suit. '*Warwick and District Recorder*. Arthur Hornblow.' He indicates the other one, in the spotless, light grey double-breasted suit. 'Photographer.'

Arthur Hornblow says nothing. He holds his whopping great camera against his chest like a shield.

'Are you two all there is?' says the manager. 'I sent out press releases to everyone!'

'Well, I don't know about everyone,' says Ed Goulding. 'We're from the *Warwick and District Recorder*. Highest local paper per capita circulation in the Midlands, mate.'

'No, no, no,' mutters the manager. 'I wanted proper press coverage.' The bubble of today's festival of back-slapping seems to have burst. Before he can protest further, he's called away by a checkout girl to a spillage emergency in the tinned goods aisle.

Ed Goulding whips out his notebook. Arthur Hornblow doesn't do anything. I get the impression they've both been covering supermarket openings for about fifty years.

'Ed Goulding, *Warwick and District Recorder*,' says Ed Goulding. 'Can we have a word? Short interview? Won't take a moment?'

'Sure.'

Pen poised over notebook. 'So, what's your name, son?'

'Tom,' I say. 'Tom Miller.'

Scribble. 'Uh-huh. And how old are you, Tim?'

'Tom. I'm fifteen.'

Scribble. 'Uh-huh. And how long have you been working as Prince George's double, Tim?'

'Tom. Actually, I'm not a "double". That's not a word we're allowed to use. I'm a lookalike. About eighteen months, to answer the question. I'm with the Blue Book Agency in Birmingham. They do all sorts. Pop stars, movie stars, sports stars. I'm their only royalty at the moment. They had a Queen, but she's in hospital with her leg.'

Scribble. 'Uh-huh. Well, you're the spitting image of him, son. What do your friends and family think about you being Prince George, then, Tim?'

'Tom. Oh, they're well used to it by now! I suppose I'm infamous all over school! I'm at Emerson High, by the way.'

Scribble. 'Uh-huh. Do they call you "Your Highness" and stuff, then?'

'Oh no, nothing like that. I just mean, everyone knows me, because of the Prince George thing.'

Scribble. 'Uh-huh. You a big fan of the royals, then?'

'Er, well, my mum is.'

Scribble. 'Uh-huh. And being Prince George keeps you busy, then?'

'Yeah. I do things like this, and the odd bit of advert work, I'm doing something most weekends. I'm saving most of the money I earn, you know, for the future. University ain't getting any cheaper!'

Scribble. 'Uh-huh. OK, thanks, Tim.'

'Tom.'

'Arthur?'

Arthur Hornblow suddenly leaps into action. Click. Crouch down. Click. To the side. Click.

'OK . . . look straight at the camera, Tim . . . Nice, nice . . . Straight at the camera . . . Nice . . . Hold up the ribbon . . . Nice . . . Hold up the scissors . . . OK, that's fine.'

They each shake my hand, thank Tim for his time and are gone before I can even register in which direction they're heading.

By now, the manager has dealt with the spillage emergency in the tinned goods aisle and returns with a placard covered in special offers.

'Have they gone?' he says.

'Yes. Just now.'

'Bastards. I wanted them to mention our fresh pasta promotion.'

He shows me to a windowless, scuff-carpeted room lined with lockers and plastic seats, with *Staff Lounge* on the door. I change out of my Prince George casual-look jacket and tie ensemble (a very close match to what he wore for his public appearance at Wimbledon last year, although costing rather less) and back into my jeans, woolly jumper and baseball cap.

I thank the manager and he smiles grimly. You can see that all the special magic has gone from his day, now, what with spillage emergencies and no mention for the fresh pasta promotion. He tells me that the cheque will be with the Blue Book Agency by the end of next week.

I catch the crowded Route-67 bus home. At least this job has been quite close to where I live. Often, you have to travel miles! Today's Route-67 bus is one of those squat, chunky ones, with 'CityHopper' swirling along the side and a driver who'd clearly rather be sawing his own leg off than driving people around on a Saturday lunchtime.

Just as you can present a realistic lookalike portrayal with the help of body language, so body language can help you stay anonymous when you want to be. I elongate my walk a little, and slump a bit, and with the cap pulled down I don't get the 'Hey, you're exactly like . . . ?' thing from anyone.

Which is good, after you've done a job, because you just want a little peace and quiet for a while.

A similar train of thought chugs through my head after most jobs, too. I sit towards the back of the bus, next to the window, with one foot up on the wheel arch, and yup, here comes the 14:22 to My Inner Monologue.

As the bus grumbles along The Parade, I think: *Why DOES Joe Public play along with it all? I'm not the real Prince George – they know I'm not, I know I'm not, but they behave as if I was. All smiles and politeness. People ask to have their photo taken with me. Weird. Nobody famous is involved. It's two nobodies standing side by side. It's all down to my facial features*. My friend Jack Baker would say it's all down to traditional British bone-idleness. That was part of his school concert routine.

As the bus lurches sullenly past the Island Road Civic Centre: . . . *Two nobodies? Am I a nobody? Who am I, then, exactly? Everyone sees Prince George when they look at me, I dress like Prince George, I talk like Prince George (nearly). So I guess in some strange way I must BE Prince George. Well, Prince George version two. Ha! Not a nobody at all!*

As the bus mutters and whines its way around the Mortensen Park housing estate: *What's the real Prince George doing now, I wonder? What's he got planned for the weekend? He's not sitting on a bus winding its way around the Mortensen Park housing estate, that's for sure! He's not got a biology essay that's got to be done by Monday, that's for sure!*

Jealous? Me? You bet I am!

Like I said, thoughts like these always seem to follow a job, the same way excessive farting always seems to follow a plate of SuperSave fresh pasta. In both cases, you simply get it over and done with, and it's gone.

I suppose it's just tiredness. All such self-absorbed musings are banished from my mind by the time I get off the bus at Hawthorne Street. I'm a happy bunny again. All's right with the world, and why shouldn't it be?

Naturally, any feeling of effervescent cheerfulness gets the edge knocked off it the minute I get home. Home tends to have that effect.

'Hi!' I cry.

Mum comes scurrying out of the dining room. 'How did it go? I want to hear all the details.' She does a quick staccato dust down of the sleeve of her puce v-neck M&S pullover. There's not a speck of anything down her sleeve, but she dusts it anyway.

The pullover goes tastefully with the skirt, which goes tastefully with the necklace, which goes tastefully with the interior décor throughout the house. My mother is a person of above-average height, above-average hair and above-average orderliness.

'It went fine,' I say cheerily.

She smiles at me silently, with the words 'Yes, and . . . ?' printed in enormous letters across her forehead.

'It went *really* fine,' I say.

She peels those letters off her forehead and speaks them instead: 'Yes, and . . . ?'

'Well . . . all the details are pretty much the same details as the details for any similar job at any similar time. So . . . for details, refer to earlier details.'

Her smile doesn't so much as twitch. I think she's assuming I'm cross that she wasn't there. I am not.

'I'm so sorry I couldn't go with you . . .' she says.

Really. I am not.

'. . . but I'd promised to help out at the school governors' meeting . . .'

Hurrah for the school governors' meeting!

'. . . and today was the only day they could all make it. So it did go OK, then?'

'Yes, Mum.'

'Good.'

She gives me a hug and a kiss on the cheek and says, 'I'm so proud of you. I do miss you when I can't be there.'

All this could lead you to think: 'Ahhh, what a great mum! She's so supportive! She's so clean and presentable! And you're being such a misery about her!'

Hold it. Freeze frame.

Some Things That Should Be Realised:

1. Relentless support, ruthless good taste and brutal tidiness can really get on your nerves!

2. Having a parent who's always *helping out* with things can really get on your nerves too!

3. She tags along to *most* of my jobs, and stands there in the crowd! And applauds! What? That's not too bad? *I've only just weaned her off the camcorder!* She's got hours of me on DVD cutting ribbons and introducing guest speakers at company sales conferences! It CAN REALLY GET ON YOUR NERVES!

4. Her name is Gladys. No, that is not a misprint.

I always get the impression that Mum's the sort of person who very nearly named me Ralph, just so that she could insist on it being pronounced 'Raef'.

True, there are far worse mothers in the world. But I don't have to live with them, do I? I have to live with this one. And this one CAN REALLY GET ON YOUR NERVES.

She stops hugging me and skips back to the dining room. I go via the kitchen, where I storm the fridge to liberate some grub.

Mum is at her enormous display cabinet. It looms over the dining room, ready to mercilessly start conversations whenever anyone comes over to eat. It's a fiesta of wood and glass, and every item in it is arranged with precision, and every item is in mint condition, and I'm trying very hard not to call it a shrine.

Mum calls it her collection. Memorabilia of royalty and royal occasions that goes back to the late nineteenth century. To be fair, there are some very rare and valuable pieces in this cabinet, including a plate with a portrait of Queen Victoria on it and a misprinted mug from the Silver Jubilee of 1977 (with the Union Jack put on upside down – most of them were recalled and destroyed, hence the rarity value). As a collection it's genuinely impressive. As a reflection of my mother's state of mind it's terrifying.

I mean, she's not a barmy obsessive. The house isn't filled with knitted models of Buckingham Palace and framed commemorative issues of the *Radio Times*. Everything is, at least, confined to this one room, and is, at least, an actual collector's item.

But it's still a shrine. Sorry, there's no other word for it. In the base of the cabinet, in the long, low cupboardy bit, are scrapbooks and press cuttings and those DVDs I mentioned. All of it covered in me.

My mother is a woman who's very keen on 'Standards'. Exactly what these 'Standards' are it's surprisingly hard to define, but in general they revolve around politeness and clarity of speech, respectability of friends and neighbours, smartness of dress and living environment, and just being a bit of a snob, basically.

She idolises royalty, mostly because she sees them as the living embodiment of these 'Standards' she's so keen on. All royalty, worldwide. But with us being Brits, naturally it's the UK edition that gets the bulk of her attention.

She has this peculiar, blinkered view of royal people as being somehow more respectable, more historically important than the rest of us. More worthwhile. An ideal to live up to. A figurehead of trust and responsibility.

(But what about all the gutter press royal horror stories? Surely it would take someone unbelievably parochial and close-minded to ignore all that? To avoid seeing the royals as anything other than regular, fallible human beings? Surely it would take someone who couldn't just ignore the proverbial elephant in the room, but ignore a whole herd of elephants, half a dozen giraffes and a lion? And yes. It would.)

Since that's her attitude to THEM, it's also her attitude to ME. I am also, apparently, more respectable, historically important, worthwhile, ideal, trustworthy and responsible than anyone else in the whole wide world. I look like a royal, I can act like a royal, therefore I practically AM royal. I am the image of the 'Standards' she holds so dear. I am the perfect son. I am a prince amongst men.

And you can't really kick up a fuss about that, can you? That's the trouble. How do you tell someone who obviously adores you that they CAN REALLY GET ON YOUR NERVES? It's not easy. It's not even possible, at least not for me.

So I bite my tongue, and I stay as Prince George, and the scrapbooks get fatter.

I'm not much of a rebel.

(Besides, the money's pretty handy. In the last year

alone I've bought myself one fabulous lightning bolt of a computer, and the building society must be thinking I'm as well-heeled as a shoe shop, what with all the cheques I keep paying in. And that's after Mum's had her percentage.)

My mother glides through domestic life with the banner of 'Standards' held high, and me held up there with it. I try to avoid thinking about such issues. It's a settled way of life, I suppose, but sometimes it's difficult to swallow.

What's also difficult to swallow is the plate of SuperSave fresh pasta I'm currently bullying with a fork. I'm hoping it was nicer when it was hot. Maybe the fridge took a dislike to it.

'Did you have this for lunch?' I say, chewing uncertainly at it as I'm wandering into the dining room.

'Yes, it was quite nice,' says Mum. She's busy polishing a Princess Diana porcelain figurine which clearly doesn't need polishing. 'Don't drop any of that on the carpet!'

Nobody with 'Standards' would drop their SuperSave fresh pasta on the carpet, now, would they? I introduce the pasta to the kitchen bin and hope they'll be very happy together.

I retreat to my room. I think about doing my biology homework, but end up thinking about Louise instead.

Oh, Louise . . .

Oh, get your biology homework done, you mad, lovesick, impossibly handsome young fool! I bet Prince George does his biology homework smack on time!

I bet he doesn't. I bet he gets a passing butler to do it for him, lucky swine. Actually, thinking about it, Prince George is a little older than me, nearly nineteen, so he doesn't even HAVE biology homework any more. Lucky swine.

I do my biology homework. It distracts my attention for a little while, but already my mind's drifting towards Monday. I know it sounds weird, but I like school. I like my notoriety. I like the way all the girls make a point of saying hello. I like the way everyone knows who I am.

Who am I? Yeh, I really AM Prince George, first in line to the throne, only son of the King and Queen, international teen heart-throb (or as close as it's possible to get)! I've got the saturnine good looks, I've got the style, I've even got the swoopy, floppy night-dark hair done to perfection.

And that's not something a lot of people can say, now, is it?

Chapter 2

I'd be perfectly happy living at school full time. I've made enquiries, but apparently there are rules about dossing down on school premises. I've argued that Prince George went to a boarding school, and that it would help with my Saturday job, but no dice.

Emerson High is a living textbook on architecture. Going from left to right along Selby Avenue:

First, there's the original Victorian bit, a gothic-looking building, all points and ornaments. It has a sharp-roofed bell tower jutting up from its centre and everyone refers to it as Dracula's Castle.

Second, attached by a covered walkway which leaks every time it rains, is a glassy box built in the 1960s. Science labs at the top, assembly hall underneath.

Third, there's a big modern chunk in front of the sports field, all sloping sections and round windows. This was only finished a few years before I started at the school.

Architecture is not part of the National Curriculum, and thus no student at Emerson High can tell you anything more about the different styles of building, how they were built or where they fit into the history of British architectural design. Me included.

Emerson High is the local 'good school'. The one which pushy parents move house to get their kids into. It's so high up the academic league tables it's in danger of falling off the top of the printout, and by hook or by crook the Head and all her staff are going to damn well keep it that way. It has a solidly middle class catchment area, which means three things:

1. Most of the parents have careers, pension plans and roomy four-door saloon cars.
2. Most of the kids are secretly dismayed and embarrassed by their parents' careers, pension plans and roomy four-door saloon cars and are therefore very interested in left-wing politics.
3. It's the sort of school where a fifteen-year-old Prince George lookalike can be popular and successful, rather than beaten up, as he would be in any normal environment.

The walk to Emerson High from home takes exactly twelve minutes. Today I'm anticipating coming up against a certain amount of amused sarcasm when I arrive, because quite a few people will have seen this morning's *Warwick and District Recorder*.

Photo: me, holding up a pair of scissors outside

SuperSave, looking like a right dork.

Headline: *Double Trouble For Tim!*

Text: *Local teen Tim Muller, 18, is a double for top royal favourite Prince George. Tim, who attends Blue Book School in Birmingham, is used to his friends and family calling him 'Your Highness'. 'I'm infamous all over school!' he claims.*

He's been a big fan of the royals for eighteen months, after another double, this time for Queen Elizabeth I, went into hospital. He's been making appearances as Prince George's double ever since! 'Everyone knows me,' he says.

Tim is using the money he earns as a double to pay for his mum's university course. 'It ain't getting any cheaper!' he declares.

Tim is pictured here opening the new Cubbington branch of SuperSave. Absent was store manager Charles Lederer.

At breakfast, I read it and snorted Wheetie Puffs across the table with mirth. Mum just snorted, without the Wheetie Puffs, and without the mirth, then clipped the piece out and filed it away. 'One hundred and nineteen words, ten factual errors,' she said in a low voice. 'I think that's a new record, even for the *Recorder*. And please get those Wheetie Puffs off the tablecloth!'

Once I'm past the school gates, it's a full one minute and ten seconds before a copy of the *Recorder* is waggled in front of me. Which is longer than I expected.

'Hiya, Timmy,' says Ellen Arden of 12B, in a voice like melting butter.

'They were overwhelmed by my sparkling charisma,' I say, turning round to face her as I walk and doing a complete about-face in the process. 'Couldn't keep their pencils straight! Minds went blank! Starstruck!'

She giggles and shakes her head. 'Riiiiight . . .'

I get to class a few minutes ahead of the bell. On the way, Amanda Dell says hi, Iris Martin says hi, Lois Laurel says hi, and Rose Loomis says hi. And I say hi back, giving them all my most devastating smile.

I mean, they adore me. I'm so sharp, so confident, so famously regal. Even their parents adore me. You can see them at sports days and school plays: that's the boy, there, the one who's Prince George, nice boy, very polite, lovely manners. Eligible.

It'd be easy to get big-headed about it, wouldn't it?

So I get to class with the usual Monday morning spring in my step, and there's a round of 'Hiya' s and 'Whacha do at the weekend, then?'s, and half a dozen more Tim jokes. Most of the others are already there. Vicky and Harriet make a beeline for me. They ask me to a thing they're having next Saturday, but I tell them I can't make it because I'm doing a photo-shoot for a Wheetie Puffs poster ad campaign.

I'm not, I just don't want to go out with either of them. I want to go out with Louise.

At first, I can't see her, but as Vicky and Harriet glide away I catch sight of her at her desk beside the window. She's reading a paperback on theoretical cosmology.

She's so wonderfully well informed. She's totally absorbed; the muscles of her face are adrift, the way they go when your attention is utterly fixed elsewhere.

She's a touch shorter than most of the other girls, and her face is a touch more contoured. Her nose ends in a perfect semicircle, and a little beauty spot adorns her cheek on a precise vertical alignment with her left pupil. Her eyes are greeny-blue, and bluey-grey, and greyey-green, and all three at once. Her eyebrows have a very slight kink in the middle, which gives her a look of permanent innocence. Her hair tumbles around her, more glowingly blond than anything that could come out of a bottle, short but wild, like a splash of water. No matter what she's wearing, her clothes cuddle her as if they can't bear to ever let go.

Louise.

She walks in beauty like the night. Is that how it goes? I can't remember where that's from. She nightly walks in beauty? No. I don't do poetry.

I did try writing her some poetry once, to show her my sensitive side. But the only things I could think of to rhyme with 'Louise' were 'help me please', 'on my knees' and 'I like cheese'. None of them seemed appropriate. I binned the poem quickly, before the hideous creature could evolve a second verse.

The only real poem I can remember is that one about tygers burning in the forest. I considered reading that one to her, but somehow it didn't seem appropriate either.

I love her.

Simple as that.

Proper love, I mean, not some adolescent infatuation. She is, of course, the most drop-dead gorgeous girl on the face of the planet. Whenever I see her, my heart skips enough beats to set off a cardiograph. One glimpse of her warms the inner corners of my soul as if a nuclear device had just detonated in my head.

But that's not why I love her. That's why I fancy her. Everyone fancies her. Even Gay Daniel in 11A fancies her. It was fancying at first sight, on my first day at this school. But not love.

That's how I know my love is real. It's grown over time. It's bloomed. And with every passing day it becomes more complete, more consuming, more electrically alive.

If only.

If only.

If only I had the nerve to tell her how I feel.

She's the only one. She's the only girl in the entire school who doesn't go just the tiniest bit gooey in the eyes when Prince George here gives her his most devastating smile.

I've tried. Often. I've turned the Prince George dial up to maximum and there's nothing. Zip. Zilch. Nowt.

It's not that she doesn't like me. We get on very well, as a matter of fact. Best buddies 'n' all that. It's simply that there isn't the feedback which comes from the other girls. It's not there, in her eyes, or the way she moves.

She doesn't fancy me back. And that's what keeps me silent. That's why I can't tell her how much she means to me. That why I pine away like a discarded puppy in the sad bit of a kiddies' cartoon film.

She doesn't love me back.

How do you tell someone who'll never love you the way you love them that they mean more to you than life itself?

She's brilliant, as well. At most subjects, but especially at science. It's one of the many qualities in her that's fuelled my love. Ultimately, she's aiming to get a doctorate in theoretical physics! Honest, she is! A brain the size of a major public building – how sexy is THAT?!

I'm quite good, academically (frankly, you have to be at this school, or you get leaned on), but I'm barely a tick in an old exercise book compared to the stellar grades of Louise Wilder.

Prince George is what I have. He's what I am. It's all I have to offer her, really. And she doesn't seem to want it.

'Hi,' I say.

'Hello, Tom,' she says cheerily, looking up from her book.

I don't manage to get so much as another word in. Allan appears at my shoulder, all polished and minty fresh.

'Guys,' he says. 'What d'you think about ankle-length boots?'

Louise and I consider for a moment.

'I have to say, I think they'd look worse than the sandals,' says Louise. 'They're cheesy, AND they're dated.'

'Damn,' mutters Allan.

Allan Snyder is on a quest. A difficult and challenging one, which is taxing his powers of creativity and ingenuity to their very limits. He is searching for the perfect out-of-school wardrobe. This week he's fretting about shoes.

'You were better off with the designer trainers,' I mumble.

'Gone right off trainers,' he says, pursing his lips (and with lips the size of his, that practically means shifting his centre of gravity). 'Too niche. Wanna be cool. Don't wanna be TOO cool, y'know. I need an overall look that's timeless, that's hip, that suits my physique. Fine line between cool and loser, y'know, and I can't afford to be on the wrong side of it. Nah, trainers won't do.'

Why he won't settle for a simple mix of shirts and trousers like the rest of us, I don't know. He just has this thing about his appearance: he wears himself like a badge. It took him a month to decide whether to use the occasional dab of hair gel or not.

I notice that Louise has flashed him a smile, and my heart is ripped asunder for a moment or two. My heart gets ripped asunder like this regularly.

As far as I can see, Allan Snyder is an obvious candidate for Winner Of Louise's Heart. Although it rips my heart asunder again to admit it.

Me versus Allan Snyder – a Statistical Analysis, first one to reach five points wins . . .

ME: Handsome, very. Prince George lookalike.

ALLAN SNYDER: Handsome, very. In that kind of cheekboned way that girls seem to like. A kissy-kissy gob (see above), good teeth.

Score: One all.

ME: Harbouring secret inner love.

ALLAN SNYDER: Incapable of harbouring anything. Couldn't hide his feelings if his life depended on it. And girls LIKE transparency. If he was any more OPEN he'd drop apart.

Score: Two–one to Snyder.

ME: Strangely fixated mother.

ALLAN SNYDER: Two older brothers, both at Oxford (that's the actual university, not Oxford College Of Dentists or anything like that!), Dad runs internet stationery retailer, Mum runs marathons for charity. Ye gods!

Score: Three–one to Snyder.

ME: Doing quite nicely from my Saturday job, thank you very much.

ALLAN SNYDER: Lives in the biggest house on Selby Avenue, right opposite the school. Not just well-off, RICH! Show me a girl who doesn't respond to THAT!

Score: Four–one to Snyder.

ME: Fine about things the way they are (except for the intense pain of the harbouring-secret-inner-love bit), a pillar of the community, decent grades, respectable, etc, etc.

ALLAN SNYDER: Doesn't give a flying monkey's about grades, respectability, or wearing non-regulation items mixed in with school uniform. Even the odd bit of internet essay plagiarism holds no fears! Show me a girl who doesn't respond to THAT TOO!

Score: Five–one to Snyder.

Game, set and match.

Makes me sick. Mr bloody Perfect, nyahh, nyahh, nyaaaaahh!

Jealous? Of course I am! I'm as jealous of him as I am of the real Prince George!

The thing about Allan is that he's all shell. Like an egg, I mean, not a crab or anything like that. He's all smooth, shiny surface – take that away and there'd be nothing left of him. (I think he gets it from his dad, the online stationer. His dad is one of those people who thinks that if he puts on tinted glasses and yellow stripy trousers it makes him a lovable eccentric. He's the dullest bloke I've ever met.)

I suppose, though, that you've got to grudgingly respect a guy like Allan. In the end, by and large, on the whole. He's perfectly comfortable with his own shiny, shallow Allan Snyder-ness. Get an electron microscope and take a look at his atoms, and I bet you every last one of them has *Property of Allan Snyder* stamped on it.

He's very much his own man, is Allan Snyder. Unlike yours truly, who is of course very much Prince George.

And this is my dilemma. This is why I have to adore Louise from afar. This is the one and only fly in the soothing ointment of my George-ness. Allan is Allan, I am the person I am. And I am Prince George.

But Louise . . .

So maybe . . . Maybe, on the other hand, I should reassess who I am. Maybe —

'Maybe something tougher-looking,' says Allan. 'Plain shirt and trousers is . . .' He wrinkles his nose and does a see-saw with his hands. '. . . unexciting. Doesn't convey action. Right, Jack?'

I haven't even noticed Jack Baker come in. He's sitting cross-legged on his desk, the toes of his huge shoes poking out over the sides, sandy hair uncombed, a vacant expression on his face.

He's been like that a lot recently, for some reason. Vacant-looking, I mean, as if he's mulling over something weird and can't make up his mind about it.

Don't know why.

'Huh?' he says, snapping to.

'Something tougher,' says Allan. 'I need to convey man-of-action.'

Jack ponders for a moment. 'Big boots.'

Louise and I both smirk. Allan just shakes his head.

'Nope, wondered about something similar a minute ago,' he says.

'A headband,' says Jack flatly.

'Mmmnnnn . . .' Allan wrinkles his nose again.

'Combat trousers.'

'Mmmnnnn . . .'

'A white T-shirt and gold medallion.'

'Mmmnnnn . . .'

'Wow, Allan, just how tough do you want to look?'

I laugh. Jack Baker is a funny guy. He's gangly and crumpled, and he has worryingly large feet. He's a guy who cultivates an air of amused indifference, one of those guys who position themselves on the outskirts of any social circle. He always strikes me as someone who's very self-assured. He is also my best friend (Louise notwithstanding).

Try this one for size. He's a GENIUS at accents, can pin them down perfectly, first time. So whenever there's a new teacher in the school, he convinces them he's from a different part of the country. The Head thinks he speaks with a Dorset twang. Our history teacher thinks he's from Belfast.

His crowning glory was Mr Truitt. Now Mr Truitt, it's true, is a bit of a pushover. If he was any softer he'd be a puddle. He arrived at the school at the beginning of this year, replacing Mr Lawford, who left teaching to make his own range of pots in a studio in Weston-Super-Mare (and who, by the way, thought Jack was Welsh).

First lesson, hi Mr Truitt, hi everyone, and we're all waiting to hear what Jack comes out with. Truitt gets around to Jack, and Jack's suddenly Australian. The rest of us are at bursting point. Truitt has an entire conversation with Jack about Melbourne, and the outback, and climbing up Sydney Harbour Bridge.

And THEN, next lesson, Jack's a Brummie! Truitt can't work it out, you can see his mind grinding to a halt. Jack's TOTALLY convincing – sorry, sir? Australia, sir? But I've never been there, sir. Are you sure, sir?

Wouldn't have worked with anyone but Truitt. Jack saw straight through the man and homed in on his weakness! Incredible!

Actually, thinking about it, Jack hasn't pulled a trick like that for a while. Don't know why. But when he does it's a scream.

Accents was a topic covered in Jack's stand-up comedy routine. The Head's very keen on fund-raisers, and two years ago the annual school concert proved to be a financial winner for the school Buy A New IT Suite fund. So the Head made the concert a termly thing. It's a sort of cross between a talent show and a chance to show off. As long as the Head approves the content, you're in. We've even had the odd teacher doing their party piece.

Anyway, at the end of last summer term, Jack does ten minutes of stand-up, and steals the show! He's a natural.

SCENE: Emerson High assembly hall; 9 July; night. Jack enters stage left, polite applause. Hits audience between eyes with a brilliant bit about regional dialects.

JACK: (as audience laughter swells) '. . . That's why you don't get French bank robbers over here. You can't be threatening in that accent, can you? "Aaand overe yoir monai". Doesn't work.'

This line was originally ruder, but watered down by Head. Leads on to section about what various languages sound like when you can't speak them (the audience is dabbing tears at this point), then leads on to section about us Brits and how we're fundamentally lazy.

JACK: '. . . That's why we've never had a revolution. Russia, 1917, freezing cold. North Korea, 1950s, boiling hot. Here, slight drizzle, we have a panic-buy on Pac-A-Macs!

We can't be bothered. We never have riots in the winter, do we? Only when the sun's shining . . . And when the sun's shining, we drive to where there's great vistas of beautiful scenery. And we sit in the car. Our biggest contribution to world cuisine? Chips. Potatoes, cut up. We're just bone idle . . .'

And of course, all through the act half the teachers in the audience are sitting there wondering why he's putting on an accent himself over his 'normal' speaking voice! Brilliant!

He's not entered this term's concert, so I guess he's working on new material. I guess.

We've known each other since primary school, believe it or not. We discovered a mutual interest in old sci-fi movies, and have been a pair of matching nerds ever since.

His mum made a mint years ago selling greetings cards featuring a repellently sentimental character called Courtney Fudge, hence the family's location in the Emerson High area. What his dad does for a living seems to be a state secret known only to his dad and the local bookie. When I was eleven I thought he might be a spy, but since then I've realised he's a professional layabout. Scruffy guy he is, too.

I've only ever been to Jack's house twice, and one of those was a ten-minute visit when he had chicken pox. He prefers to keep his family well away from people he likes, as if somehow The Baker Effect will leak into the environment if not tightly controlled. Come to think of it, he prefers to keep well away from his family himself.

His parents are like their house: semi-detached. For the majority of any twenty-four hour period they, and Jack, avoid each other's presence, and for the rest of the time they throw hissy fits at each other across the dinner table.

Not that he talks about his family much. What I know I've pieced together from clips of information here and there. Which is fine. It's up to him, isn't it? He's entitled to say nothing, if he wants.

Still waters run deep, they say, and that's certainly true in Jack's case. It's that cultivated air of amused indifference I mentioned, that social ambiguity, that detached self-assurance. I reckon it's his darker side which makes him such a great stand-up comic. They say that about comedians, don't they?

Meanwhile, Allan Snyder wanders off to try the idea of combat trousers out on some of the girls. Louise returns to her book. I talk to Jack.

'Top Five Most Gorgeous Women In TV Adverts,' I say.

'Yeh, needs an update,' says Jack, thoughtfully. 'The woman who kicks bad guys' butts for a Nuttie chocolate bar.'

'Yes. One. Girl who runs out of shampoo in the shower.'

'Definitely. Two.'

'Girl driving economical but sporty new Volkswagen to the ice-cream shop. Three. No question.'

'Three. Woman using Clairmont hair colour to miraculously transform her lifestyle.'

'Before or after?'

'Before.'

'Yes. Four.'

Before the lucky winner of fifth place can be revealed, the bell for registration clonks and Mrs Lovelady stalks in. The bell at the end of the corridor has clonked instead of rung for as long as anyone can remember. Nobody knows why.

We all slope away to our desks without another word. You don't get far in this school without learning how to slope away from Mrs Lovelady.

Fate has played a blackly comic joke on Mrs Lovelady's surname. Fate has also played a blackly comic joke on her physical appearance, her attitude to anyone under the age of thirty, and her tiny little husband.

Having said that, she amazed us all last term. Big Henry Hathaway broke his leg playing rugby, a really nasty fracture in the tibia that broke the skin. Blood everywhere, Big Henry's screaming like a baby, two other guys faint at the sight. Mrs Lovelady's the ref, and not only does she stop the bleeding with her tracksuit top, she cradles Big Henry in her arms and calms him down until the ambulance arrives. We'd all assumed she was powered by bitterness, but it turns out she has a heart after all. She just hides it well. Like I said, she amazed us.

Adjusting the considerable weight of her glasses on her freeform nose, she drops her briefcase into the drawer of her desk from shoulder height, sits, thuds an armful of papers down in front of her, adjusts her chair, locks the drawer, pockets her keys with a jangle, adjusts her chair again and picks the topmost sheet of A4 off the pile. She picks up the gist of what it says and throws it at us.

'Tom Miller. Louise Wilder. Jack Baker. Allan Snyder. Apparently two members of the Greenson College team have contracted a tropical disease and have had to pull out. That school is withdrawing from this year's finals. You four now qualify, as closest runners-up.'

She takes the register. Wide-eyed with delight, I look at Louise. She's wide-eyed with delight, too. I look at Jack. He's also wide-eyed, although whether it's with delight or shock I'm not quite sure. I can't see Allan from where I'm sitting, but I've got the vaguest feeling he just might be wide-eyed with delight as well. The bell clonks for the first lesson of the day. We stay put. It's English with Mrs Lovelady.

'Edgar Allan Poe,' says Mrs Lovelady, 'and his state of mind, our new topic is the connection between the work of four nineteenth and twentieth century writers and their mental health, stop doing that at the back, Richard Breen . . .'

I'm still wide-eyed with delight.

What?

It's only friendship and romantic entanglements which bring the four of us together? Oh noooo. It's not that simple. It's not that easy. The four of us are the reigning UK Inter-Schools Ski Champions.

Chapter 3

This school has a SKI team? This school is located in the West Midlands which, unless the atlases have been making a big mistake here, is not known for its mountains.

Quite right. And a ski team sounds a bit posh even for Emerson High, but we have a ski team because of two factors: firstly, because we have the rather terrific Snow Globe nearby in sunny Birmingham, and secondly, because of Miss Annabel Norris.

OK, imagine everything going all ripply now. All black and white, or something similar. Here's a flashback.

Way, way back in ye olden days, waaaaaaaay back in the distant mists of ancient time, all of three years ago, there was a new teacher at Emerson High called Miss Annabel Norris.

Miss Annabel Norris was, until the year before that, the Next Big Thing in the world of winter sports. The UK isn't exactly bursting at the seams with bobsleigh champions and speed skating superstars, but Miss Annabel Norris was an exception to the unwritten rule that all downhill ski event finalists have to have names full of Z's and W's.

She won half a dozen European championships, she won a couple of world championships, she won a gold and a silver at the Winter Olympics, and she did it all despite the obvious handicap of being British. She was the golden girl of UK sport. She got standing ovations at boring ceremonies in which rugby players with necks thicker than their waists looked awkward in dinner jackets.

And then, during a practice session in Switzerland, she broke both her legs, her left hip and two lumbar vertebrae. The driver of the snow plough said he never even saw her coming.

Several months later, out of hospital and in need of a job, she went back to her original career as a teacher, and ended up on the staff of Emerson High.

Enter four kids who were also new to the school, four kids with terror in their hearts at the thought of entering secondary school, and brand new uniforms which had just that little bit too much growing room in them. Miss Annabel Norris was their form tutor.

No sooner was the school year started than a skiing club was formed. The Snow Globe had just opened: real snow, real slopes, all indoors. Miss Annabel Norris soon had about a dozen club members piling into the school minibus on a Friday afternoon.

Over time, those club members dwindled to four

regulars – hey, ohmygosh, it's them same four new kids with the embarrassingly roomy blazers! Jack Baker! Ta-daa! Louise Wilder! Ta-daaaaa! Allan Snyder! Ta-DAAAAA! And me!

We stuck with it because we found we were good at it. And we were good at it because of Miss Annabel Norris. She picked us up when we skidded headfirst into the snow. She sparked our enthusiasm when we watched footage of what the world champions could do and felt like giving up. She negotiated hefty discounts from the people who ran the Snow Globe.

And, to cut a long story short, we won last year's UK Inter-Schools Ski Championship.

Now, to be fair, the UK Inter-Schools Ski Championship doesn't have all THAT many entrants each year. There isn't some secret underground network of ski-mad schoolkids just itching for the chance to compete on a national level. The schools that take part are either Scottish (after all, they're next door to real mountains), or clustered around the three or four Snow Globe-type places that exist in the rest of the country. There are half a dozen from the Milton Keynes area, a couple from near Poole, some from a place in Wales with several L's in it, and us.

The competition is funded by some official sports council thingummy whatsit. It's basically a way of identifying potential UK competitors for all the events that Miss Annabel Norris won during her short but spectacular career. Ten schools are in the finals, forty finalists in all.

For six years, Cargavern High in Glasgow had an unbeaten and apparently unbeatable run as champions. They've got a full time trainer (!) and sponsorship from a chain of butchers' shops (!!). They were the kings of the under-eighteen winter sports world.

Until the Emerson High squad came along. Whahayyyyy! We snipped the title from their grasp in the last event of the three-day competition.

They were gutted. GUTTED!

I think that was when I finally fell in love with Louise. She took calculated risks to shave a few seconds off her downhill run: pulling tightly into the natural slopes of the course, and taking a straight line over bumps when a slight veer to one side would have kept her more stable on the snow. That took the sort of guts I'll never have.

We returned to school to a hero's welcome. Well, four heroes' welcomes! We are now, officially, the Head's pride and joy. I think she's intending to have us trademarked as The Standard Of Excellence For All Other Students To Achieve.

We returned to school, and Miss Annabel Norris promptly announced she was leaving. She'd been offered a job coaching the actual England squad.

She left at the end of last summer term, two days after Jack's brilliant showing at the school concert. Not that there's a connection, of course, I'm just putting things in context!

The qualifying events for this year's championships were held last term. We didn't have our mentor any more, but we were damned sure we weren't going to let her down. We practised twice a week, three times a week after half term. Jack took over the job of teambuilding and did a bloody good job. We were fit, we were skilled, we were ready.

We missed out on a place in the finals by three and a half seconds. We were gutted. GUTTED! Cargavern High were ecstatic.

We thought it was all over. Until right now. It seems we have a title to defend.

All through Mrs Lovelady's English class, the four of us are paying no attention whatsoever to Edgar Allan Poe and his tragic battles with his inner demons. I don't even have to glance at the others to know that the same three thoughts are working their way through our brains:

1. How the hell are we going to pull off a second win without Miss Annabel Norris?
2. How the hell are we even going to compete effectively when we've let up on the practice sessions following our shock defeat?
3. How the hell did two members of the Greenson College team manage to contract a tropical disease like that?

Feeling pressured, anyone?

Meanwhile, a fourth thought is going through my brain, all on its own. A thought about Louise. A thought that maybe, possibly, you never know, this time the white heat of competition might help to bring Louise and me closer together.

Chapter 4

The white heat of competition is driving Louise and me further apart than ever. I am more desolate and wretched than an afternoon in Coventry.

The four of us got called to the Head's office, out of lessons, just so that she could tell us how chuffed she was about the competition and how much the entire school will be rooting for us.

Thanks.

It's now two weeks since we heard we'd qualified after all, and three weeks until the spring term break, when the entire school will apparently be rooting for us.

Thanks.

The four of us have spent a total of six evenings and one Sunday morning at the Snow Globe. Or, at least, three of us have. One of us, who will remain nameless – JACK BAKER – has spent a total of five evenings and no Sunday mornings at the Snow Globe. With no explanation whatsoever.

The rest of us are feeling a bit cheesed off with Jack. Since Miss Annabel Norris left, he's always been the one who rallies us and keeps our spirits up, but in the last couple of weeks, he seems to have lost the ability to communicate in anything other than grunts and shrugs.

'You weren't at last night's practice,' I say.

He grunts.

'Couldn't you make it last night?' says Louise at lunchtime.

He shrugs.

Maybe he's just busy working on new material for his act. But given the peculiar mood he seems to be in, maybe that's unlikely. Jack's always been a person with Something On His Mind. Still waters, and all that. Even so, we're cheesed off with him.

Jeez, we're all under pressure here, Jack. The rest of us aren't going to pieces.

Anyway. Enough about Jack. He's annoyed me. More about Louise.

I really thought that these last couple of weeks would mean the two of us spending more time together. Socially, I mean, not just belting down the Advanced Slope at the Snow Globe. But after our practice sessions are over, we're all so shattered that the best we can manage is a half-hearted wave and a 'see you tomorrow'.

There aren't really any tactics to talk about, as such, not in this competition anyway. Three days, three events: day one is cross-country, day two is the slalom, day three is the downhill. All against the clock. There's not much you can say, strategy-wise – there are only so many times you can go over the phrase 'move like hell, pass the finish line, then stop'.

School's busy, too, so I don't get nearly enough opportunities to talk to Louise there either at the moment. I considered feigning total confusion over the essay we've got to do for Mrs Lovelady, re: Edgar Allan Poe and his assorted personal miseries, and asking Louise for 'help', but decided against it for two reasons:

1. What with Louise being a certified genius, any appearance of poor intelligence on my part is bound to look unattractive.

2. I'm not finding the subject of Edgar Allan Poe and his assorted personal miseries all that gripping anyway, and the thought of spending even more time on it isn't exactly exciting.

I'm feeling utterly stuck. I can't even scrape together an excuse to see her over the weekends. Last Saturday I was being Prince George to promote the refit of a men's clothing store in Kidderminster, and on Sunday I was being Prince George to declare open a dog show at the Seven Year Arena, Cardiff. (Went brilliantly. Got a couple of really nice freebies from the clothing store, actually.)

The Saturday before, I got roped into going to Vicky and Harriet's party after all. They gave me the distinct impression that they'd invited the whole class, meaning Louise included, and they damn well hadn't. It was all an excuse to wedge me in a corner for the evening and talk about Prince George and how I'm world famous and how all four of their parents were away for the weekend.

On the Sunday, Mum forced me at tongue-point to help her repaint the living room. She seems to think that if our house doesn't get redecorated every so often the local council will slap a 'Condemned' notice on it and Channel 4 will start making shocking documentaries about the filthy people who live in it. She's like a DIY dalek: 'Redecorate! Redecorate!'

The living room is now Wild Orchid. That's yellowy-white. Yuk.

The aching intensity of my love for Louise is made all the more unbearable on the following Tuesday. That Tuesday is a day of two unexpected revelations, one poetically beautiful, one like a stab in the chest with a rusty spike.

The poetically beautiful one first.

Tuesday is almost warm. The sagging clouds, which have been hanging like wet laundry over the town since the beginning of the year, shuffle aside for a few hours to let a woozy patch of sunlight through.

At morning break, pupils actually stay in the open air out of choice. I find Louise, legs outstretched, sitting alone on the line of wooden benches to the side of Dracula's Castle. They face the trees beyond, from which you can see everything that's going on across the playing field, but Louise is looking upwards, at the sky. Her book is folded up in her arms, one finger marking her place.

'Hi,' I say. 'Wha'cha up to?'

'Hiya.'

She smiles, and I sit next to her. Not RIGHT next to her, of course, but just-good-friends next to her. At a distance of approximately twenty centimetres. Familiar next to her, comfortable-with-each-other next to her, not invading-your-personal-space next to her. Not girlfriend–boyfriend next to her. I've become very good at being beside Louise without giving the game away.

'Just thinking about things,' she says.

'Like what?'

She smiles again. 'Like what I've been reading.' There's the tiniest hint of embarrassment in her voice. She knows I know she's been reading about physics, and I know she knows I know she's been reading about physics. Again. And she's expecting me to give her the tiniest hint that I'm pulling her leg about it. But I decide not to.

'So what are you reading?' I say.

'About the mathematical clash between general and special relativity and quantum mechanics, and how it's all resolved by string theory.'

I think for a moment or two. 'All the individual words, I'm fine with. It's how they get arranged in that sentence that confuses me.'

She laughs, tilting her head back to return her gaze to the sky. 'String theory is just . . . elegant. The most elegantly brilliant thing in the world.'

'Correct me if I'm wrong,' I say. 'But we haven't studied any of this in physics, have we?'

'Don't you ever read around subjects? Don't you want to explore beyond the borders of what we get taught?'

I think for a moment or two.

'No.'

'Well you should. It's where all the interesting stuff is. The useful stuff.'

'So this theory about bits of string is both brilliant and useful?'

'Not bits of string, dummy. Strings. Fundamental, one-dimension loops.' She fixes her gaze on the clouds, and the leaves swaying at the tops of the trees. 'You can't see them, or even measure them, not properly. They're billions of times smaller than the smallest particle, and they resonate. They vibrate in patterns, in harmonies, and they explain the formation of the sub-atomic world. They resonate at different frequencies, and the differences are what creates the forces that hold the hysterical weirdness of the sub-atomic world together. Gravity, electromagnetism, the strong and weak forces. Their resonances explain the binding of particles into physical matter, and the matter becomes the clouds, and the trees, and us, and the Earth, and the universe. All of it different, but the same. Built from the simplest things. Trillion upon trillion of them, flowing together, working to the simplest rules, adding up to everything. The gigantic and the microscopic, all in tune with each other.'

For a second, just for a second, I see what she means. The world as infinitely complicated music. It's weird. Startling.

This is the poetically beautiful revelation I mentioned.

'And that's string theory, is it?'

'Kind of,' she says, with a manic grin and comical wide-eyes. 'Can we talk about Kaluza–Klein Theory now? That's got multiple spacial dimensions in it!'

I think for a moment or two.

'No.'

You know, I think perhaps I was wrong. About the moment when we won last year's finals. Maybe THIS is the moment when I finally, completely fall in love with her. The moment when I see the crystal clarity and vision of her mind.

I tell her my brain's overheating. I need to talk about something trivial instead.

Meanwhile, the stab-in-the-chest-with-a-rusty-spike revelation is coming up any minute now.

'Something trivial,' she says. 'Er . . . the intense pressure of the imminent ski finals? The difficulties of our current English assignment? Things you've done as a lookalike recently?'

'They're not trivial.'

'I was being ironic.'

'Sorry.'

'Hair! Let's talk about hair!' she says, comically batting her eyelashes at me.

'That's girly,' I say quietly.

'Hair brushes? Hairspray? Conditioner! Ooooh, conditioner! Yeeeehh!'

'So these strings, then . . .'

She laughs. And at this precise moment, she moves closer to me.

Closer. To me. It's indisputable. I am acutely aware of these things, and she definitely, clearly, undoubtedly moves closer to me. At least three centimetres. At least!

My heart starts racing. But I don't react.

Play it cool! Play it cool!

'I thought I'd go to the cinema at the weekend,' I say, playing it cooler than a snowman's fridge.

'Yeh? I'm going tomorrow night, with Allan.'

In an instant, a rusty spike strikes deep into my chest. Every last drop of energy drains out of me.

My heart has stopped. But I don't react.

'With . . . Allan?' I say.

'Yeh. It's something with explosions and car chases. Not my usual thing, really, but he asked, so I'm going. Might be fun.'

'Like . . . a date?'

'Er, well, I suppose so, yes. Why?'

'No reason! No reason! I just . . . didn't know you were . . . going . . . on a date . . . with Allan. That's all.'

The rusty spike is twisting, twisting.

I knew it! I was right, I knew it! I've always seen this was a possibility. I always knew this day would come.

Louise and Allan.

Suddenly, we can hear the bell clonking inside the school building. The flow of pupils and teachers around us speeds up. Louise and I make our way back to class. We talk about Allan's quest for the perfect wardrobe. With a giggle, she says she'll suggest brightly coloured socks to him. I feel like suggesting a range of pullovers with Backstabbing Underhand Swine knitted across them.

I don't understand it. I don't UNDERSTAND.

Yes I do. For all the reasons I've already explained. Because he won the Statistical Analysis five points to one.

It's just . . . not fair.

Oh, come on! Come ON! It's just a date. Just a date. Just a couple of friends going to the same place, at the same time. Together.

It doesn't mean anything. At least, it doesn't HAVE to mean anything.

People go on dates all the time, don't they? Doesn't have to mean anything. It's just a date. With him, and not me.

I don't UNDERSTAND!

There's an incident from our past. My past, and Louise's. It suddenly looms large in my mind.

Last winter, before Miss Annabel Norris left the school, the team went on a trip to France, a ski resort called Lausalles, near the Italian border. Nice place.

It was a half-holiday, half-training-camp sort of thing. A week of skiing and staying up late and wishing we were in slightly more up-market accommodation.

On the day before we're due to fly home, Louise and I find ourselves at the top of one of the advanced slopes just below the tree line, on our own. Jack's taking photos for the school newsletter, Allan's off shopping and Miss Annabel Norris is deep in conversation with the local instructor, a man who is clearly overwhelmed by her Olympic credentials.

So. Being experienced skiers, and responsible young adults and all that, Louise and I set off down the mountain. And within a couple of minutes, we're racing each other, and having a laugh, and basically not paying attention. We're off piste and skirting around a wooded area before you can say 'snow goggles'.

We hit a wide, open patch of very soft snow. Very fine, powdery snow, the sort that looks like the picture on your granny's biscuit tin and can kill you in minutes. You think I'm joking? Snow ain't just snow – you get all sorts of it. The powdery sort is what you usually get in avalanches. It doesn't cling together, you see, it isn't compacted enough. And if you start walking through it, you can sink right down to your neck.

The thing is, maybe we shouldn't have stopped. If we'd kept going, with the snow skimming around our knees and our skis out of sight underneath somewhere, we might have steered ourselves back on to the proper slope. If we'd known where we going.

But we didn't. So we stopped. And once we've stopped, moving about becomes difficult.

The mountains are fabulous. We can see for miles,

through air that's so sharp and clean and clear it's like an invisible knife edge. The gorgeous dark blue of the cloudless sky gradually fades as it nears the sun. It's so quiet and peaceful.

And the two of us are up to our waists. We're absolutely still, not daring to do anything for a moment. There's nobody else in sight. Thirty metres above us are trees, and above the tops of the trees we can see the top of the mountain, starkly jagged against blue. Below us, the snow curves gently downwards, out of sight.

'Oh crap,' says Louise.

'It's OK,' I say. 'C'mon, we know what we're doing. We can work our way back.'

'What if we can't?'

'We can. C'mon. We can.'

And slowly, very slowly, we do. It sounds peculiar to say that snow can be frightening, right? But believe me, it can. When you can't get a proper grip on it, when you can feel the delicate balance of it beneath you, even through thick socks and chunky boots and skis. When you can sense that you're stuck fast and adrift at the same time. It's an unnerving sensation, I promise you.

We struggle along in our ski gear, with our puffy, primary-coloured coats shining in the sunlight and our hair getting steadily sweatier under our sporty helmets.

We must look a right sight, I tell myself. A couple of total twits, I tell myself. I say it over and over again to myself, mostly to distract my mind from other thoughts.

Thoughts about sinking. Into snow. Into glistening whiteness up over our heads. Into some deep cleft in the rock below us that we don't even know is there. Into cold beyond endurance. Into untraceability. Into death.

Louise keeps getting panicky. It seems to overcome her in short waves. I manoeuvre alongside her as best I can and talk, talk about anything to keep her mind distracted too. Here and there I grip her under her arm and pull her.

She is astonishing. You can see that fear is gradually filling up her head, but she keeps going. She gets the better of it. We move an arm, a leg, an arm, a leg, one after the other, forward a bit, and forward again, shifting ourselves up the slope.

And eventually I can feel the snow getting more solid. Each movement gets us a little further than before. We rise a little higher.

And suddenly, we're OK. We're closer to the trees and we're back on the non-terrifying snow.

We sit, with our skis sticking up in the air, breathing heavily. We pull our helmets off. Bad hair day!

'What a couple of total twits,' I gasp.

She smiles.

We agree on something. We will never, ever, not in a million years, tell anyone about this little incident. Never. We're OK, we got out of it, nobody ever needs to know.

Come to think of it, maybe I was wrong about the moment when we won the championship last year, and the moment when she opened my mind to the infinite complexity of the universe. THIS is the moment when I fall in love with Louise. Sitting here, under the trees. When I see her inner strength. She was scared out her wits, but she never let it beat her. She never gave in. And I love her so much for that.

'Is my helmet hair as bad as yours?' she says.

'Worse,' I say.

We trudge back to our chalet. We eat an enormous dinner and pretend to be interested in the designer shirts Allan's bought.

Now, you'd think that an event like that would have a more lasting impact. You'd think that an event like that would have brought us closer together, Louise and me? We have a secret, and secrets glue people to each other like nothing else in the world.

But no. Not only do we not talk about the incident to other people, we don't talk about it to each other, either.

Her attitude towards me doesn't appear to have changed. But I love her all the more. Now I've seen what determination she's capable of, I love her with every last bit of love at my disposal.

Perhaps I should have said something there and then, once we were back safe and sound. Perhaps I should have chosen my moment, and said: 'Look, I don't know about you, but for me things have changed. Let's go and have a pizza and a chat.'

But I didn't say anything. And soon, the moment for saying something kind of passed by.

Who am I kidding? Even if I'd decided to say something, I'd have spent for ever 'choosing my moment' as usual, wouldn't I? And the moment would have passed by anyway.

And now, today, she's GOING ON A DATE WITH ALLAN! I thought, when she moved closer to me on the bench – and she DID move closer to me – that maybe . . . but now she's GOING ON A DATE WITH BLOODY ALLAN!

Calm down!

It's just a date.

It doesn't mean anything.

It really, really, really doesn't mean anything.

Of course it means something, you blithering idiot!

I'm in a mental whirlpool for the rest of the morning. I wash up on the shores of normality at around lunchtime, feeling dizzy.

The four of us converge on the same table in the canteen. Jack and I arrive first.

We're both having the egg and chips. I've mostly stopped being annoyed with him.

It occurs to me, as we sit down amid the clattering jumble of the canteen, THE place at Emerson High where plots get hatched and alliances get forged and opinions get boggled at, that here's the perfect opportunity to get someone else's perspective on the Louise-and-Allan problem.

In the two seconds it takes to sit, I consider the following scenario carefully: I am in love with Louise; Louise is not in love with me; my love for her has created a certain turmoil inside me – something unexpected and entirely unprecedented – which is crying out to be resolved; I cannot resolve this turmoil myself; the logical solution is to confide in my oldest friend and ask for an impartial judgement.

By the time my bum hits the bench, I have reached a sensible conclusion.

'Hi,' I say.

'Hi,' says Jack.

'Top Five Science Fiction Movies Of The Twentieth Century,' I say.

'Good one,' says Jack.

What?

Me, TELL Jack? Oh, come ON! I can't tell Louise, so how the hell can I tell Jack? He's my oldest friend! There are certain lines that you just don't cross. We're MALE! It doesn't work like that!

Jack gazes up at the pock-marked ceiling while he thinks. He's like that for a couple of minutes, gazing away, the corners of his mouth turned down, as if either he keeps losing his train of thought or else the ceiling is particularly fascinating today.

'2001,' he says eventually, '*Close Encounters, Metropolis, Forbidden Planet*, the 1931 *Frankenstein*.'

'Does *Frankenstein* count?'

'I'm using the Brian Aldiss definition of science fiction.'

'Of course. Fair enough. Not *Star Wars*?'

'I'd rather slice my droids off with a lightsabre.'

'Quite right.'

'Here's a related one. All-time Top Three TV Series About Spies.'

'*Alias, Mission: Impossible, Spooks*, no contest.'

'No contest.'

We eat. Louise appears, followed (literally) by Allan. They're both having the pasta salad.

We chat about the state of the canteen, and the way the practice sessions are going, and our chances in the competition, and the gossip about those three kids from 8G who – whisperwhisperwhisper – and Mrs Lovelady's absolutely hiiiiiiiideous shoes, and the likely daily routine of MR Lovelady, and once we've stopped sniggering we're back to the competition again.

'Yeh, well,' says Jack, chasing a chip around his plate as if it's got legs and a strong will to survive, 'perhaps we should think of a plan for nobbling the Cargavern High squad. That'd give us our best chance.'

Allan slaps down his fork. 'Not going to win with that attitude, are we? Huh?' (It's what you'd expect some character in a TV movie to say, one of those two-dimensional characters you can't remember ten minutes after the credits have rolled. But that's exactly what Allan is like. So that's how he talks.)

Jack looks at him. I mean, really LOOKS at him.

'And what attitude are we going to win with then, Allan? What attitude can we adopt that is suddenly going to sweep us to victory, Allan? A change of attitude, is that all we need, is it, Allan?'

Allan picks up his fork and twirls it between his fingers for a few seconds. His fleshy lips are doing a brisk tango together. A smart comeback here will require a certain depth of thought, a certain blossoming of personality.

'Tell you what,' he says at last. 'Turning up. That'd help.'

'I told you, I was busy,' says Jack quietly. Suddenly, he looks kind of pale and deflated. As if all his blood has decided it wants to move bodies but can't find the exit.

'Jack?' says Louise. 'Are you OK? Are you feeling all right?'

With a sudden splat, Jack flings that last surviving chip against the table. He pulls himself to his feet in a single, angry jerk. The loud screech of the chair legs against the scuffed lino makes people turn to look. Those who don't turn at the sound of the chair turn at the sound of his voice.

'Of course I'm OK!' he cries. 'What's the bloody matter with people? What's this sudden interest everybody's got in whether I'm OK or not? Of course I'm OK, don't be so bloody nosy!'

He marches away. If real life had a sense of drama, there would be a sudden darkening of the sky through the windows and a low rumble of thunder. But there isn't. The only sudden darkening is around Jack, as he walks through the sunlight, past dozens of mildly curious faces. The only low rumble is coming from Gay Daniel of 11A's stomach, on the table next to ours.

Louise stares at me for a moment. 'Do any of us know why he's in such a bad mood recently?' she asks.

Apparently not. She stands up and follows Jack. Allan sits there shaking his head slowly.

'Some people,' he says. 'Can't take it. Bit of pressure, fall to pieces. If he loses the competition for us, I'll kill him.'

The only thoughts of killing I'm harbouring are ones about killing Allan. The low-down, scum-scooping, girl-snatching, back-stabbing . . .

He suddenly scoots around the table and sits next to me. His gaze does a quick three hundred and sixty degree flick to check for ears.

'Tom, mate,' he says, in a conspiratorial tone. He has such a chummy air about him that I keep expecting him to start selling me dodgy DVDs. 'Can I confide in you?'

I. BEG. Your pardon?

'Er . . .' I say. Long pause. 'Sure.'

'New thing for me. Emotions are a bit . . .' He weaves his hand around in the air. 'So thought I'd spill the beans. You're a solid bloke. Need a heart-to-heart, you know?'

I am speechless. Quite literally, without speech of any kind.

'One good thing,' says Allan. 'Result of this competition. Reckon the pressure is bringing Louise and me closer together.'

What?

WHAT?

NO! That was supposed to happen to ME! To MEEEE!

He purses his lips and does a slow, wide-eyed nod, eye-brows on the move like scalded caterpillars. 'Yup. Have to say, getting reeeeeally keen on Louise. Know what I mean? Really keen. And. Think she's getting to feel the same about me.'

There goes that nod again.

No.

No.

It's not true . . . It can't be true . . .

'Going on a date with her. Pretty pleased with myself, actually. Was assuming the only way she'd ever go out with me was if she was trying to make some other guy jealous, y'know? Wouldn't bother me if she did, mind you. Done the same myself in the past. And I'd still be going out with her, right? Anyway, on this date, thought I might make a move. What do you think?'

My mind appears to have got a new operating system. It keeps crashing and forcing me to reboot. I may have lost data. Is he asking ME . . . for . . . about LOUISE?

This guy is ALL SHELL. Everything gets reflected out-wards.

'I . . . think . . . no . . . way . . .' is all I can eventually push out past my teeth.

'Too soon? Yeh, maybe. Hmm. Good call. Don't want to mess this one up. Yeh, I'll wait till the weekend. Thanks, mate.'

He gives me a slap on the shoulder, stands and picks up his tray. Then he remembers something. 'By the way,

Louise suggested brightly coloured socks. Really not sure, myself. Can't help thinking it doesn't sound right?'

'No,' I say flatly. 'They'd be great. I think you may have found The Look, there.'

'Hmmm,' says Allan, wrinkling his nose. 'Not sure.' He wanders off.

A short, high-pitched belch comes from somewhere behind me. 'Beg pardon,' says Gay Daniel of 11A, at the next table. 'I seem to have the most terrible wind today.'

Chapter 5

What the hell do I do now?

The woman I love is going out with Allan bloody Snyder. I am tortured by reminders that he won the Me versus Allan Snyder Statistical Analysis five points to one. This is a guy who defines himself by what brand of toothpaste he uses. This is a guy who has no opinions that aren't cut and pasted from magazines and websites. And he STILL beat me five points to one! Game, set and match.

There's really only one thing I can do. Late that night, lying awake worrying about Louise and Allan bloody Snyder, I realise that I've only got one card to play, and that I'm going to have to play it to the max.

I'm Prince George. I AM Prince George. I know it hasn't appeared to impress Louise up to now, but perhaps I wasn't full-on enough.

I know I was having doubts. Thoughts about reassessing the real me. But I can't simply BECOME a whole new me, can I? I am Prince George and Prince George is me. And that's that, right?

Perhaps there were one or two minor flaws in my interpretation of the guy: after all, Louise is a certified genius, is she not? She's bound to spot things like that, and perhaps it's things like that which have been putting her off?

So. I will be a winner, in my own way. As much as Allan bloody Snyder is in HIS. What else can I do?

The next morning, I bound out of bed despite the fact that I've had far too little sleep on account of all the worrying. I have renewed hope.

I turn on the charm. From the very moment I first gaze at my fabulously George-like face in the mirror, I am in character. And I stay that way.

At breakfast, I even eat my Wheetie Puffs in Prince George styley, even though I've never actually managed to see footage of the guy eating anything. I improvise, and I'm pretty damn sure I do a good job. Mum approves of my efforts, as demonstrated by her warm but very slightly disturbing smile.

I even smarten up my school uniform. My shoes get a polish, my tie gets attentively straightened, and I place a crisply folded handkerchief in the breast pocket of my blazer, poking out just enough to be noticeable but not enough to look stupid.

At school, the overall package has an instantaneous effect. I get 'Helloed' and 'Hiya-ed' even more than usual. I even get 'Good morning-ed' by a couple of teachers. All the time, I never once break character. I don't force it, though: I don't adjust my voice as much as I would on a job, just give it a bit of a shine. But I do keep all the gestures and body language, including the most minor items.

I surprise myself with how smoothly I can keep it going for a sustained period like this. The longest I've ever needed to do it before was about four hours, at a Women's Institute charity thing in Newcastle-Under-Lyme. I suppose it's simply a question of wearing my public persona the way most people wear a pair of jeans. It's almost second nature, these days.

And with me BEHAVING like Prince George as well as LOOKING like Prince George, the girls are giving me looks that would melt rock and dropping hints that are heavier than a cartoon anvil. And it's FUN! Most of the boys don't really remark on the change, partly because a shift in body language isn't top of their agenda anyway, but mostly because they're well used to my George-ness and know all about its girl-related effects.

One or two of them pass comments, such as: 'Bloody hell, Tom, leave some space for the rest of us' or, 'You got a big job coming up or something?' One or two assume I'm trying to attract the undying devotion of Vicky and Harriet. Vicky and Harriet are clearly assuming that too. Ellen Arden of 12B sweeps by me outside the art room and says 'Hello, George' in a voice like Belgian chocolate. Now THAT'S never happened before! Nobody's ever actually addressed me as George before! Not at school, anyway.

After a couple of days of giving them all the full George treatment, the effect seeps through to the girls' parents. Three times, at the end of the afternoon, as we're all starting to head off home, I spot mums in cars leaning over and talking to their daughters about me. They look and half point, and think I haven't noticed. Lois Laurel's mum gets almost insistent. Lois spins momentarily to glance in my direction, her hair doing that swooshy thing which makes her look like a L'Oréal advert. For the briefest of instants, embarrassment masks her face. She gets into the car and it moves off. I know what the mums are saying because the next day Rose Loomis gets exactly the same little pep talk, but instead of leaping into the passenger seat she trots over to me.

'Hey, Tom.'

'Hi.'

'Listen, do you fancy coming over to my house tomorrow night? I could do with some help on the English project. This Edgar Allan Poe psychology thing is more of a mystery than his stories!'

I'm tempted. I really am. Rose is a nice girl, although if she was any more toothy you'd worry about her being hunted by ivory poachers. The thing is, I'm sure she's being completely honest when she says the English project is giving her trouble. She's no Louise in the brains department. I resolve to keep myself focussed.

'I'd love to, Rose, but I've already promised my mum I'd help her recarpet the stairs.'

(Sharp answer. There's nothing that puts a girl off a boy faster than her thinking he does what his mum tells him. Although, for some reason, girls' mums think the exact opposite. Anyway . . .)

'Uh, OK,' says Rose. Her smile says it's not OK at all, that it's very disappointing. For a minute I feel like a total louse, and as she walks away I fight the urge to call her back, and run up to her and say how sorry I am and hold on to her tightly. I HATE making anyone feel like that.

But! I've resolved to keep myself focussed.

All this parental attention is buoyed up by the fact that the real Prince George is very much in the news at the moment. There's been coverage of his forthcoming university course, due to start in October; there's been coverage of his triumphs in his school's rugby league team; there's been a documentary on Channel Five about just what an all-round terrific A1 top-notch bloke he is. No parent could have missed it all. And I've assiduously kept myself up to speed with the lot of it.

However, there is one failing in this whole plan, one 'What Is Wrong With This Picture' thing. Just one tiny little problem.

Louise hates me.

Let me think carefully for a moment here. Is 'hates' the right word? Has she really gone off me to that extent?

Yes, I think she has. My Prince George persona has been flawless. Flawless. Every other girl in the school: bowled over. Louise: hates me.

I thought at first . . . No, to be more accurate, I HOPED at first, that it was a twinge of jealousy. I hoped she'd noticed just how much of a double-points bonus I was scoring with the likes of Vicky and Harriet and Ellen Arden of 12B. I hoped.

But no such luck. My flawlessness seems to have backfired worse than a broken exhaust on a ten-tonne truck. I have been Prince George when I've talked to her, I have been Prince George when we've sat at adjacent desks during history, and I have been Prince George when we've simply been in the same room and not even talking or comparing history notes or anything. And all I've got from her is a series of silent looks. These looks have been, in order of appearance:

1. The 'Why Do I Sense You Are Different?' look.
2. The 'Am I Supposed To Be Impressed?' look.
3. The 'Well, I'm Not' look.
4. The 'I Hate You' look.

What's more, the Allan Snyder situation has got worse. Louise has now gone to the cinema with him TWICE, and they've also eaten – together, alone! – at the Emperor's Palace, only the most up-market and frankly delicious Chinese restaurant in the entire West Midlands.

I don't know what to do. I just don't know WHAT to do!

I've played my last card. I've played my ONLY card. And it's lost me the game.

Then, hey, guess what happens?

That's right!

My mother phones the *Warwick and District Recorder*.

'Huh?' I say at breakfast the following morning. My spoon dangles, dripping milk into my Wheetie Puffs.

'It'll be good publicity,' says Mum. She eyes the dripping milk. The whole concept of dripping bothers her terribly, but this time she manages to stay on-message: 'Your team's done brilliantly to get into the finals again. You all deserve recognition.' Her fixed facial expression of indomitable optimism goes into battle with my wrinkled-up facial expression of complete bewilderment.

'Muuuuum,' I protest. 'You mean it's another chance to drum up business for me.'

'Exactly,' says Mum. 'It'll be good publicity. The Head thinks it's a terrific idea too, I called her last night.'

'Muuuuum.'

'The four of you will need to take your ski gear into school today. It'll look better for the photo, so you need to ring the others straight away.'

'Muuuuum.'

I can't tell which facial expression has won the battle. Neither of us has moved a muscle.

So ten minutes later I'm ringing the other three, and four hours and fifteen minutes after that, during lunch break, we're standing outside Dracula's Castle in full competition ski gear and feeling like right losers. We're being stared at by every passing kid and teacher. Some of the jokes we're having thrown at us would still sound juvenile coming from a six-year-old. And the ones we're getting from the kids are no better. We're all clutching our skis to our chests and not talking to each other. The atmosphere is a tiny bit tense.

Eventually, the Head comes scuttling along. She's wearing the sharply cropped dark grey dress that she keeps in her office for official occasions. She's all smiles and heavy foundation, and she keeps bobbing her hair about as if it were a group of Year Sevens in need of discipline.

'Lovely turnout, ski team,' she announces, slightly out of breath. 'Fabulous. Aren't the people from the *Recorder* here yet?' She whips out her lippy and smears her mouth into a shade of red which makes you want to post a letter into it. 'Lovely,' she says, to nobody in particular.

Suddenly, two very tall men stride out of nowhere and introduce themselves to the Head.

'Ed Goulding,' says the one in the spotless, dark blue double-breasted suit. '*Warwick and District Recorder*. This is Arthur Hornblow.' He indicates the other one, in the spotless light grey double-breasted suit. 'Photographer.'

I let out a long, low breath. For goodness' sake, hasn't the *Warwick and District Recorder* got any other reporters?

'Super,' says the Head.

The interview does not go well. They call me Tim, they're only interested in the Prince George angle and every question gets addressed to me, no matter what I say. Except for one. Ed Goulding turns to the others and says, 'So, you three, what's it like being at school with Prince George?'

'We're not,' says Louise. If her voice were any more tart you could stick a pair of fishnet stockings on it.

I can feel, actually FEEL, psychic waves of irritation emi-nating from the other three. There's a sarcastic comment brewing behind Jack's eyes that I'm terrified to unleash. He's been simmering uncomfortably, all unspoken com-ments and brooding looks, ever since he stormed out of lunch the other day.

'Wonderful,' announces the Head. 'Would you like a quote from me? About the school? And the team? Or a photo?'

'Ahh, no thanks, cheers, got what I needed,' says Ed Goulding. They are gone before I can even register in which direction they're heading.

The Head tells us all how well we've done and scuttles back to her office. We slope off to pack our skis away, and change back into our uniforms.

'Nice one, Tim,' says Allan.

'It's not my fault!' I protest.

Louise takes a quick poke at the carefully positioned handkerchief still peeking out of my breast pocket. 'Isn't it?'

'I am SO looking forward to next week,' says Allan.

The sarcastic comment behind Jack's eyes has reached boiling point. I can see an enormous, dripping bubble of verbal spite forming, ready to burst. I brace myself for a violent strike from his mighty blade of sardonic wit.

He looks at me sadly. 'Prat,' he mumbles.

That's it, is it? Oooh, there's real effort went into that one, eh? I expected something a little more satirical from Jack, but no, apparently not.

What IS going on with him recently, huh? What IS his problem? He's beginning to annoy me again.

Louise and Allan are walking ahead.

There is one week to go until half term. Which means there is one week and two days to go before the start of the UK Inter-Schools Ski Championships.

I am not happy. Not. Happy.

Chapter 6

There are thirty-seven teachers at Emerson High. Some of them are more or less OK on a good day, some of them are genuinely nice people who are interesting to listen to, and some of them make you want to jump head first into a barrel of live piranhas.

Given all that, what are the chances that picking a couple of them, at random, would turn up two piranhas? Not all that great, I don't suppose. Louise would be able to give you an accurate probability. So the fact that it's two piranhas who are accompanying us on our trip to the finals in Scotland is just one more helping of bad luck to add to all the other things which don't exactly bode well for the competition.

The staff had a lottery. The UK Sports Council Thingummy Whatsit that's funding the whole event are paying for three adults, as well as the four of us. So the staff had a lottery. They all wanted to go, since none of them were about to turn down the chance of a freebie, and the winners were: (drum roll) . . .

Mrs Lovelady! (Oh whoopee! Yey!)

Mr Truitt of the history department! (Oh joy! Ding!)

Mrs Lovelady, despite the carefully hidden depths of injury-related tenderness she displayed on the rugby field last term, counts as one of the piranha group for reasons which should be obvious by now. Mr Truitt, on the other hand, you'd think was a nicey-nice little lambkin until you spend more than ten minutes in his presence.

The trouble with Mr Truitt is, he's never off duty. He has to educationalise everything. To death. As if his brain will implode if he doesn't keep puffing it up with pointless analytical irrelevance. Until you want to grab him by the shoulders and shake him and shout, 'Stop it! Stop it, you boring, irritating man!' right in his face.

He's a tall bloke, as thin and stretched as the nerves of the people he talks to. To overcompensate for his peculiarly weedy physique, he wears baggy corduroy trousers, baggy corduroy jackets and baggy shirts which look like they ought to be corduroy even though they're not. And all of it is brown. Never the same shade of brown twice, but always brown. Chocolate brown trousers, mud brown jacket, SuperSave Choco-mousse brown shirt, etc, etc. You get the idea. All brown.

He has one of those faces which permanently looks like it's about to sneeze. Nostrils angled upwards, eyes at half-mast. Even his wavy (brown) hair seems to be on the verge of a shudder.

I have plenty of time to contemplate Mr Truitt's oddities during the many months it appears to take for our party to go from check-in desk to departure gate at the airport. I have all this time to myself partly because the other three members of the ski team are hardly talking to me, and partly because I keep walking around the duty-free shops to avoid my mum talking to me.

My mum is the third adult. My. Mum.

We didn't HAVE to have a parent come along. It wasn't obligatory. Teachers would have been enough. But no. Mum has to start dropping sixteen-tonne hints about her work on the PTA and how much she's HELPED OUT with raffles and school fêtes this year, and then, oh what a surprise, the Head invites her to go.

So I wander the duty-free aisles, trying to suppress feelings of crushing embarrassment. I do have one short conversation with Louise, though. It goes like this:

Louise: (quietly) What do you think's bothering Jack?

Me: (shrugging shoulders) Dunno. He's been a right misery.

Louise: He hasn't spoken to me since he blew his top in the canteen the other week.

Me: He also said not to be so nosy. Is it really our business? He can be a misery if he wants to, can't he?

Louise: Tom! He's our friend! He's your friend especially. That's not a very nice attitude.

Me: Well, it's not very nice him being a right misery.

She shakes her head and walks away. End of conversation. Another brilliant example of The Tom Miller Method For Repelling Louise. I sigh and go back to perusing the airport bookshop, but there's only so long you can spend pretending to take an interest in heart-tugging family sagas or thrillers with submarines on the cover.

We're all getting a bit more lively and a bit less mind-numbingly bored by the time we're all in the departure lounge. We're all trying to find seats far enough away from a screaming four-year-old and wondering what those stains on the seats are.

Mum and Mrs Lovelady are talking, slightly too loudly, about government education policy, the role of secondary education in society, and how nice and normal Prince George comes across on telly. When Mrs Lovelady gets on to the complete history of her sister's Mysterious Stomach Problem I hum quietly to myself so as not to hear.

Meanwhile, Allan has taken the opportunity to wander around the departure lounge with Louise, as if it were a sun-kissed meadow full of buttercups or something, the low-down, back-stabbing snake. Jack is standing by the huge windows, looking out at the aircraft as they taxi back and forth.

So, doesn't that leave just me and Mr Truitt, sitting next to each other, with me unable to escape?

Correct.

'Don't you think it's fascinating, Tom, observing the

hurly-burly of activity going on around us in situations like this?'

'Yes, sir.'

'It makes you wonder how the Victorians would have reacted to the age of mass transport and jet aircraft, doesn't it?'

'Yes, sir.'

'You see, I think the Tudors or Stuarts, or even the later Georgians, wouldn't have welcomed technology, had it developed earlier. They had a very different mindset.'

'Yes, sir.'

'Of course, even thirty years ago, we would all have acted quite differently in a situation like this.'

'Oh, shut up, sir! Just leave it! You're like a dog with a bloody bone!'

No, of course I don't really say that. I say, 'Yes, sir'.

I must be looking helpless and in need of distraction because a woman in clumpy high heels, who's been marching about the departure lounge for ages, suddenly stops and talks to me with her head cocked to one side. She's very round and very dark, covered in rings and necklaces, with a floral smell that follows behind her like an obedient puppy.

'Excuse me, young man, but did you know you look JUST like Prince George?'

'Umm, I have been told so, yes.'

'He's quite a celebrity at our school,' says Mr Truitt. Thanks, Mr Truitt.

'Are you really?' she twitters. 'You're one of those look-likey people, are you?' Light bounces off her big, round glasses. 'Of course,' she says, 'I'd have them all shot, myself. Royalty, I mean, not the look-likey people.'

'Phew,' I say.

'No offence,' she says, as she marches away again.

'None taken.'

Hearing this, Mum suddenly jerks in her seat, as if someone has hit her round the head with a rolled up newspaper. She hurriedly restarts her chat with Mrs Lovelady about how wonderful the school's A-level results were last year.

'You know,' says Mr Truitt, 'the monarchy has often been an institution without mass popularity in this country. In the twentieth century, it was only after the efforts of —'

At this point my brain goes numb, and the next thing I'm aware of is a muffled female voice coming from the overhead speakers. Everyone hurries down the clanking, breezy metal tunnel to the aircraft, amid mumbles of 'At last' from everyone except the four-year-old who was screaming, who starts bleating, 'Are we there yet?'

Mum scuttles to my side. 'Keep well away from that woman in the glasses. What a nasty piece of work.'

'She's entitled to an opinion.'

'Yes, but what a horrible opinion!'

We're seated in a block near to the back. Nobody has compared seat numbers, so we're all still hoping to be sitting next to someone we like. Mum is next to the woman with the glasses.

I'm thinking: *Louise, please let me be next to Louise, please, please, please, if there is any justice or compassion in this world, please let me be next to Louise.*

I'm next to Mr Truitt.

Louise is next to Allan.

Nobody has the social temerity to say anything or ask to change seats. Except Mum. She deliberately restarts her conversation with Mrs Lovelady about the National Curriculum and corners the woman with the tinted glasses into being polite and offering to swap places.

At least I have a window seat. I'm thinking: *Can this trip accumulate ANY more bad luck, bad omens, bad karma? Can ANYTHING else go according to my worst nightmares?*

Mr Truitt is a nervous flyer. His fingers are going tappity-tappity on both arms rests and his jaw is doing something similar, drumming out a Morse code from his teeth that would probably translate as, 'Aargghhhhh!' Why the hell did he put his name into the teachers' lottery hat in the first place?

'You all right, sir?' I say.

'Oh, yes yes yes yes, Tom, fine,' he chatters. 'Isn't it interesting how all these different systems work on these planes? Air conditioning, lighting, emergency oxygen. Thousands of moving parts, all functioning at once.'

They haven't even turned the engines on yet. A very attractive stewardess, smartly ironed into a purple uniform which looks like it was specially designed to suit nobody, bustles over to Mr Truitt.

'Can I get you anything, sir?' she says sweetly, with an Aussie twang. She has to use one severely manicured hand to keep her purple cap on. 'A glass of water?'

'Oh, no no no no, I'm fine, thank you,' says Mr Truitt.

'Are you a nervous flyer, sir? Is there anything I can do to help?'

'Oh, no no no no. Just had a heavy breakfast, that's all. Tell me, are the emergency oxygen systems automatic? Or do we have to open a hatch or something?'

The slow, low whining of the engines starting up begins to throb through the cabin. As the stewardess talks calmly to Mr Truitt, I use the minute or so before the fasten seat-belts sign comes on to grab Mum's copy of the *Warwick and District Recorder*. I haven't brought a book with me because, of course, I'd been hoping so much that I'd be chatting to Louise on the way, that all other possibilities slipped my mind.

Until we're at fifty thousand feet, I pay as much atten-tion as possible to reports, such as *Pensioner's Terrier Wins Dog Show* and *Residents' Fury At Road Scheme*, and as little attention as possible to the quietly gibbering maniac sitting next to me. I think the stewardess is beginning to wish she'd missed the flight.

On page five of the *Recorder* is a photo of me and the ski team. We're pulling assorted faces which might pass for smiles, and pointing to our skis like complete idiots.

Tim Leads School Team To Victory

The Emerson High ski squad have won the World Schools Championships for the third year running. Pictured here are team captain Tim Mellor (12), Louise Wilder (15), Jack Baker (15) and Allan Snyder (16).

Tim is well known as the town's Prince George double. He'll be appearing as Prince George in a special skiing event in Scotland this week. 'It's so great to be at school with Prince George,' says fellow teammate Louise. The school's head teacher declined to comment.

I start tearing the page into several million shreds. The plane is cruising along calmly, and Mr Truitt is doing like-wise. I think the stewardess has slipped him a couple of brandies.

I notice Jack, who's on the other side of the aisle, slouched next to an empty seat and scribbling distractedly on the back cover of *Flying Hi: The In-Flight Magazine Of Diamond Air*. Before I'm really thinking about it, I find myself gripping the seat in front to haul myself upright, and edging past Mr Truitt, mumbling an apology.

I plop myself down in the empty seat and give Jack a nudge. He doesn't look up.

'What?' he mutters tonelessly.

'Wha'cha up to?'

'Nothing.'

He's doodling cubes and line-shadowed corners. To one side is a column of figures dotted with pound signs, and a list of what looks like the contents of his room at home. He notices me looking. 'Mind your own bloody business.'

I almost head back to my seat, but my short conversation with Louise at the airport suddenly pops into my mind.

I try again. 'Jack?'

'WHAT?' he spits instantly.

'Look, er, I don't want to be nosy, but —'

'Oh, why don't you just **** off!'

Hmm.

I spit out the odd **** myself. Regularly. So does Jack. So do we all. But you can tell when a **** is just what-you-happen-to-be-saying, and when it's meant as something else. And this **** is meant as something else.

I almost say, 'What's wrong?', but that sounds such a feeble and embarrassing thing to come out with. There's an awkward silence between us. Now he's realised that I'm wondering what's on his mind, he's stuffed the magazine back into the seat pocket in front of him and is tapping his biro on his knee. He's deliberately looking anywhere except at me. I think he wants me to **** off.

But he's obviously agitated about something. I try to figure out what it might be.

'Jack? You a nervous flyer like Truitt?'

'No,' he says firmly.

'Have you seen the state Truitt's in? Think yourself lucky you're not sat next to him like me!'

I decide to bite the bullet and do what Louise would tell

me to do. I'll be, er, Supportive and, umm, Understanding. And other girly things.

'Try this one,' I say. 'Top Five Pizza Toppings To Last A Lifetime. I'll start. Pineapple, prawns —'

'Will you get lost? I'm busy.'

'Look, if you're frightened of flying, you should have said so. It's OK. Really. None of us would have minded. Pineapple, prawns —'

He suddenly turns and stares straight at me. 'Go! Away!'

I pause, and let out a snort or two. 'OK, sod ya, then. Be like that. I tried.'

I stalk back to my seat and stare out of the window for a while. Below the white wing of the plane is a smooth, endless expanse of cloud, glowing under the bluest of skies, and for a moment I'm reminded of the beauty of Louise's universal vision.

I go back to ripping Mum's issue of the *Warwick and District Recorder* into a million pieces. Jack stalks off to the loo for the next twenty minutes, and it's pure chance that an angry queue doesn't form outside, or that Mrs Lovelady doesn't start demanding to know where Baker's got to. Eventually, I hear the stewardess tap on the door sharply.

'Sir? We're about to begin our descent, sir. You need to return to your seat and fasten your safety belt.' She's NOT having a good day. Jack comes past me a minute or two later, face like a small furry animal who's just read an article which puts it at the top of the endangered species list.

The aircraft descends in slumping, engine-whining stages. Mr Truitt starts humming at each movement to conceal his whimpering.

Once the aircraft comes to a halt there's a rush for hand luggage and the exits, which Mr Truitt leads. Mrs Lovelady jabs him in the shoulder as he's tugging his battered brown case down from the overhead locker. 'Get a grip, Brian,' she growls. 'You're representing the school here.'

Lockers click open and clack shut, everyone shuffles and bumps into each other, and on the overhead speakers the stewardess thanks us most sincerely for travelling with the airline today and is completely ignored. From somewhere up ahead comes the din of the screaming four-year-old yelling, 'I want to go home now.'

Chapter 7

The minibus that runs groups of tourists back and forth between Monroe airport and the Hotel Del Coronado, Glenforben, drives along a narrow, upward-sloping road which runs between lines of trees. Then it crests a small hill to give us our first sight of the hotel itself.

I say 'drives', but it's more like 'hurtles'. The enormous bloke squashed behind the wheel is, it turns out, the hotel's barman. He's already driven to the airport twice today to pick up school groups, and once to the nearby railway station, and after he's dropped us off he's back to the airport again. He keeps looking at his watch and flicking the sweat off his bald head.

I am feeling pretty chuffed with myself, because this time I AM sitting next to Louise. I had to make a flying leap on to the minibus and all but elbow Allan out of the way to do it, but I've done it.

'Glenforben,' I say. 'Sounds like a character in a book

with a submarine on the cover. Glen Forben, nuclear technician.'

'Maybe it's gossip,' says Louise. 'Glen 4 Ben.'

'Could be. Looks nice around here, anyway.'

I get the impression that the landscape wouldn't like being referred to as nice. From the look of it, it would definitely prefer to be described as 'hard' or 'implacable', and would rather be turned into a car park than be anything less than 'rugged'. Tall, sharp trees spring out of wide, flowing banks of heather and low shrubland, leading up craggy hills and rocky outcrops to peaks shining with fresh snowfall. It's spectacularly beautiful.

'By the way,' I whisper to Louise, 'umm, I think you might be right. About Jack. I think something's going on.'

She's about to say something when she notices we've arrived. 'We'll talk later,' she whispers. It's not a request, it's an order.

The minibus brakes sharply on the hotel's curling forecourt. The barman wriggles quickly out of the driving seat and hauls open the luggage hatch on the side of the vehicle. Once the four of us have unloaded our stuff, we stand looking up at the hotel admiringly.

It's got a kind of late nineteenth century look about it. There's a long, two-storey building, which wouldn't look terribly impressive on its own, but at one end of it is a very large, rounded section, with a very tall, two-tiered conical roof. Little windows jut out at regular intervals around the cone, and at its apex is what looks like a small observation deck, topped off with a flagpole. It's easily the most interesting-looking hotel I've ever been to.

'Why's it got a Spanish name?' says Allan.

'Why not?' shrugs Louise.

'Do you think there's a place in Spain called Hotel Glasgow?' I wonder out loud.

Jack is hovering behind us, keeping himself to himself. Everyone else is involved in a mass conversation around the minibus, in which the two teachers and my mother are saying that there's a suitcase missing and the barman is saying there isn't. Four normal, full-grown adults are having trouble establishing how much luggage they've got between them. The barman is sweating profusely and jabbing his glasses back up his nose.

Mrs Lovelady detaches herself from the argument and slaps a wad of papers and tickets in my hand. 'Here, Miller,' she barks. 'You're sensible enough. Go and get us all checked in while I sort this idiot out.'

The four of us scuttle into the hotel, glad to be out of the way if Mrs Lovelady's about to sort someone out. The hotel foyer is high ceilinged and circular, with leafy plants and tall-backed leather chairs dotted about.

'This is lovely,' says Louise.

Jack wanders over to one of the chairs and settles himself down, and Louise and Allan do likewise. I approach the long, shiny Reception desk, at which a long, shiny man is standing.

As I'm approaching, he looks up and sees me. And in a

nanosecond, in a split-nanosecond, in the tiniest slice of time it's possible to get, two distinct things happen:

1. The long, shiny man thinks he's got Prince George walking towards him. I can read it in his face. He suddenly gets exactly the same look that some people get when I'm out on a job. This kind of hey-that's-him stare. Only, because this man doesn't know me, and doesn't know I'm a lookalike, naturally he assumes I'm the real, genuine, bona fide Prince George. Well, you would, wouldn't you?

2. I decide to go along with it. That's my mistake. Just there. Thing Number Two. The thing I shouldn't have done. I have no excuse for it. In the one nanosecond that I have in which to make a decision, I make a bad one.

I act on instinct alone. Instinct pulls me back to what I know, and to what I feel safe with.

I reason to myself thus: Allan is closing in fast on the affections of the woman I love. The only card I have to play is still the Prince George one, but so far, that's been a dud. However, aha! Attaining some of the INFLUENCE of the real Prince George might tip the balance back in my favour. If I could gain some of his real-life AUTHORITY, some of his CLOUT, then THAT might impress Louise, surely?

Consider possible consequences? Me? Nahh.

All this happens in that one tiny splinter of time. And one tiny splinter of time later, my Prince George persona is back to full volume. I adopt the walk perfectly for the last four steps up to the Reception desk. The desk is well out of earshot of Louise, Allan and Jack.

'Good afternoon,' I say cheerily, presenting the bundle of tickets that Mrs Lovelady handed me. 'How are you today?'

The man is about fifty or so, in an immaculate dark blue suit, with an oval face and gelled-back hair. He blinks a couple of times and grins broadly, as if his features were being pulled on wires from behind his head. 'Good afternoon, sir,' he says, in a clipped, cultured Scots accent which Jack would have no trouble imitating whatsoever. 'I, umm, I heard on the grapevine that you might be back in Glenforben soon, sir, but I assumed you'd wait until the refurbishment at the Grand was finished.'

That point about the grapevine doesn't really register with me at the time. If only it had.

All I realise is that luck is on my side. 'No, actually, I thought I'd use this schools' skiing competition as cover. I'm travelling under the name Tom Miller.'

'I see, sir, very ingenious if I may say so, Your Highness. I'm so glad I happened to be at Reception for your arrival, sir. I am Mr Fenton, the general manager. Do please call me Frank.'

'Delighted to meet you, Frank.'

And Frank is delighted to meet me. He couldn't be more delighted if he tried. Possibly because he thinks he's got one over on the Grand. That grin of his is on the point of touching ends at the back of his neck.

He takes the bundle of tickets from me. 'I hardly need bother with all this, sir, of course, but you know how it is, formalities and so forth.'

'No problem, Frank. You're doing a terrific job. This place is lovely.'

'Thank you very much, sir. I must say, sir, that it's refreshing to find a personage of your stature, sir, checking into a hotel himself. We had a rather well known film star here last year, sir, and she would only communicate with the staff through her personal assistant.'

'Oh, that sort of thing is SO tiresome, Frank, I agree. No, I like to do these things myself. I'm very much my own man.'

'Of course, sir,' says Frank. 'And, umm, the three young people sitting over there, sir . . . ?'

'Are friends of mine, Frank, travelling with me. We'll be doing some skiing, as you can see from our luggage. My staff are just outside.'

'Of course, sir, security and so forth.'

'Er, quite, yes.'

He flips through the tickets and taps at the terminal that's just below desk level. 'Emerson High, sir?'

'My staff have to construct cover stories down to the tiniest detail, Frank. Helps stop the press tracking me down.'

'I see, sir! I had no idea that such precautions needed to be so thorough.'

'You can't be too careful these days, Frank.'

'Indeed not, sir. Umm, I see that since we didn't know about the cover story, sir, that we've booked you into a set of standard rooms. But now we're in full possession of the facts, and so forth, naturally I'll upgrade you all to our premier suites.'

'That's very kind of you, Frank, much appreciated. Although, er, it's just me and the three over there who require the posher rooms. The others can stay in standard.'

'Sir?'

'We've got to think of the public purse, Frank. The civil list is still paid for by the taxpayer.'

'That's very commendable, sir,' he says with pursed lips and a couple of blinks. 'I'll sort it all out for you, sir.'

'Thank you.'

He leans forward slightly. 'And, naturally, any Room Service expenses incurred by yourself and your travelling companions, sir, will be waived.'

'Really?' Now it's my turn for a couple of blinks.

'Naturally, sir, in view of this being your first visit, sir, which I hope will be the first of many, sir. I do hope that you find the accommodation and service of the Del Coronado every bit the equal of the Grand, sir, if you get my drift, and so forth.'

'I do get your drift, Frank, I do indeed.'

'Thank you, sir.'

Now it's my turn to lean forward slightly too. 'And, umm, while we're all staying here . . .'

'Sir?'

'. . . I would appreciate it if you'd help us maintain our cover story. Do please treat us all as if we really were from a school in the West Midlands called Emerson High.'

He holds up his palms and cocks his head in deference. 'Say no more, sir. Or should I say, Mr Miller?' He grins and does a theatrical wink.

'Excellent, Frank. You're a star.'

The rest of our group comes struggling into the foyer. Everyone has their luggage except Mr Truitt. I can hear the screech of the minibus departing for the airport again.

'My staff,' I whisper to Frank. 'The very neat woman is my PA. The very aggressive-looking woman is my body-guard, don't upset her whatever you do. The man in brown is from MI5, armed to the teeth.'

'Good grief. They look so ordinary, sir. You'd never guess who they were, would you, sir?'

'All part of the cover story, Frank. See you later.'

I hurry over to the others, bearing room keys and stamped paperwork. Mr Fenton hurls a few orders into the room behind the Reception desk and half a dozen uni-formed hotel staff drag themselves away from their tea break and escort us all to various parts of the hotel.

The four adjacent rooms allotted to me, Louise, Jack and Allan are big. Really BIG. They're near the top of the circu-lar section of the hotel, and even though they're packed with TVs, home cinema systems, gleaming en suite bath-rooms and little orange bottles of shampoo, there's still enough space in them to run around, jump up and down and squeak with joy.

Louise, Allan and I stand by the tall sash window in my room, looking out at the fabulous view of the mountains. Jack went to his own room ages ago.

'How the HELL did you blag this?' says Allan.

'Well, Mr Snyder, I simply appealed to the manager's commercial sense. I told him we're the team that's tipped to win, that this hotel could get a lot of good publicity out of us once we've won, and seeing as how these posher rooms weren't already being used, and blah blah blah.'

'So now we've GOT to win,' says Allan. 'Like it! Incentive! Good move!'

From Louise's level gaze, I'm sure she's spotted the truth, but she's saying nothing. There's the faintest shadow of a smirk on those adorable lips, though. I think I've impressed her. I'm sure I've impressed her.

Me: One, Snyder: nil!

And so, while I've got the advantage, I move in for the kill. 'And!' I announce. I do a dramatic pause. 'The hotel is paying for Room Service.'

'No WAY!' shrieks Allan.

'I think the manager's a bit of a ski fan,' I say. 'He's so chuffed to have all the teams staying here, it's easy to talk him into giving us a few extras.'

Allan whistles. 'I'm going to my room NOW! I'm ordering everything NOW!'

And he's gone. Louise passes by me, very close. She's struggling to control that smirk.

'What a persuasive guy you are . . . *Tom* . . .'

She knows EXACTLY what I've done. Half of her is genuinely impressed, half of her is appalled. Or that's how it looks to me. The balance shifts across her face from moment to moment. For a second, her expression darkens, and I think she's about to say something highly critical. But she changes her mind.

At the door, she stops and turns back, one hand delicately gripping the handle. 'Once I've unpacked, we'll have that talk about Jack, OK?'

'OK.'

But of course we don't. By the time we've unpacked and stopped being smug about our rooms, we're all summoned to a meeting with the competition organisers at which all the teams (except the two who haven't arrived so far) are able to meet each other. It goes on FOR EVER.

This year's Cargavern High team, our main rivals, are looking as scornfully superior as ever. They're identically tall and wiry, and one of them has got weird lines shaved out across his all-but-bald head. They all seem to have had special coaching sessions in How To Sneer At The Opposition. Most of the competitors, thirty or so of us, chat together in that stilted way you get when you're being forced to be sociable, but the most anyone can wring out of Cargavern High is one of those inverted up-nods you see exchanged between people who know they ought to be polite but who don't want to be in the same room together.

Anyway, like I said, all this goes on FOR EVER. And then the final two teams turn up, accompanied by the hotel's barman/minibus driver, who stands in a corner dabbing the sweat off his face with a sleeve. You'd think he'd personally carried the lot of them all the way here on his back.

So when the last two teams arrive, we end up going through half the introduction thing with the competition organisers AGAIN, and everything goes on FOR EVER MORE, and once we're utterly fed up and we've reach the END OF TIME we're allowed to go.

All the teachers rush off to the bar, followed by all the parents, followed wheezily by the barman. Mum goes too, but she doesn't rush. Rushing is vulgar. She merely walks at a slightly increased velocity. Meanwhile, the pep-talk meeting has so dampened the spirits of all forty competitors that most either sit around grumbling or head back to their rooms.

I want to drop hints to the Cargavern High team that their four rivals have got posher rooms than them (mostly because that could be the only thing we beat them on hands-down this week) but I don't get the opportunity. What I DO get the opportunity to do is feel teeth-grindingly jealous! Louise's unparallelled loveliness is not only getting a great deal of attention from members of other teams, it's also prompting Aaaallan to put his hand around her waist and so mark her as his own personal territory! The vile, slime-sodden toad!

And she doesn't object! Not once does she take a diplomatic step to one side to assert her independence, or carefully disentangle herself from his arm under the pretext of going to talk to someone. I want her to give him a smack in the mouth and tell him what a vile, slime-sodden toad he is. But she doesn't.

Naturally, I say nothing, and Allan doesn't know what I'm feeling, and Louise doesn't show anything either way. Is she punishing me, for pulling my Prince George trick?

I stick close to the pair of them. It makes no difference. Half my nervous system is screaming, 'Get him away from her!' and the other half is screaming, 'Run! Run for your life! Don't endure this torture any more!'

With all this going on, it's a while until I notice that Jack has wandered off again. It's a while later, when I'm curled up in bed and brooding over the length of time it took me to subtly chaperone Louise and Allan all the way to the doors of their rooms, that I suddenly remember I still haven't spoken to Louise about Jack.

And I think to myself: *She's probably suddenly remembering it too. No, she's probably asleep already. Or not. She could have decided to have that talk right now, and be sneaking out of her room, tiptoeing along the corridor to my door! The girl of my dreams could be sneaking out to see ME! Perhaps she approves of my Prince George trick after all! She could be tapping quietly at my door any second!*

Or . . .

If she can sneak out to see me, she can sneak out to see HIM! But why should she? What freebies has HE got her lately? But then, why SHOULDN'T she? She didn't object to that arm, did she? Did she?

Suddenly, I hear dulled footsteps in the thickly carpeted corridor. With my heart lurching in eight different directions at once, I fling the covers off the bed and scutter over to the door.

Opening it veeeeery slowly, I peek out. I don't know what time it is, but it's late. The lights along the corridor are dimmed. Big, globular wall lamps send out a soft glow along neutral, cream-coloured surfaces.

There's a figure. A male figure, at Louise's door!

I must be more tired than I think, because it takes me a second or two to realise that it's Jack, and that he's at his own door. I try to calm down.

As Jack idly hunts through pockets for his key, his phone emits a low warble. He snatches it from his pocket and stabs at it with a thumb. 'What?'

Jack usually leaves his phone on speaker, like I do. It's much more sci-fi. The corridor is so quiet I can just about make out a scratchy phone-voice saying, 'Jack. You didn't call . . . ?' Jack shuffles around on the spot and I don't catch the rest.

Jack just stands there. He slots his key into the lock and then just stands there again.

'What do you WANT, Dad?' he says quietly.

He shifts the phone from hand to hand and I miss most of what's said, but then the scratch-voice says '– because I phoned your mother earlier on and I had to tell her . . .' (I can't hear this bit.)

'More lies, then,' says Jack quietly.

His dad's voice rises to what must be a shout at the other end of the phone. 'Listen, young man, I am fed up with your foul moods!'

'What do you bloody expect, Dad? All this crap of yours has been doing my bloody head in!'

His dad starts to say something, his voice dropping into an imploring tone, but Jack cuts him off with the press of a button. The door slowly clicks shut, and Jack is on the other side of it.

I return to bed.

Jack's family is hardly an oasis of peace and harmony. There's nothing odd about him arguing with his dad. But something is going on. I must, must, MUST have that talk with Louise. First thing in the morning. Definitely. Without fail.

Chapter 8

Of course, I don't. I really mean to, but I don't.

Call it the excitement of staying in a posh hotel miles from home. Call it the wow factor of discovering over breakfast that the hotel not only has its own sauna, gym and jaw-droppingly overpriced gift shop, but also its own unisex hairdresser's, swimming pool and jaw-droppingly overpriced coffee shop. Whatever you choose to call it, my talk with Louise about Jack goes right out of my head.

Until Louise reminds me about it, and by then we're all caught up in the preparations for the start of the championships at ten o'clock and this, that and the other.

'Lunchtime, yeh?' says Louise.

'Definitely,' I say. 'Without fail.'

We're prompted to renew our determination to talk by the way Jack looks this morning. Last night, he LOOKED fine. But this morning he looks awful.

He looks like he hasn't slept. None of us actually SAY

anything to him, of course, and nobody actually DOES anything which might draw attention to Jack's dishevelled appearance.

Except my mother. As our party gathers with the other teams in Reception, waiting to walk en masse over to the nearby ski slopes, she places a hand on his shoulder and peers at him as if she's sneaking a look at his face around a corner. He's drawn and hollow-eyed, with a slumped, beaten-up air around him that reminds me of news bulletins about natural disasters.

'Bright and ready for the off, are we, Jack?' she says. She picks a bit of fluff off his collar, which would seem a little less prissy if she wasn't the only one in the room wearing something formal and tweedy, with matching woolly scarf and gloves, instead of something padded and thermally-lined like the rest of us.

Jack stares at her as if her voice had been a noise in his head. And this is when I finally realise that the 'something' which is going on with him is something serious, more than just an argument with his dad. There's an accumulation of oddities now. He's really not himself any more.

Because Normal-Jack would *say something*. He'd make some ego-slicing remark that Mum wouldn't spot at first but which would reduce the rest of us to concealed giggles.

This isn't Normal-Jack any more, bad moods aside.

'Sure,' he says.

I look for Louise. She's talking to Allan over by the Reception desk. The Cargavern High squad are limbering up already, and huddling together to talk tactics. I can't remember the last time the Emerson High team talked tactics. I can't help feeling we're ever so slightly screwed.

We stride out to the slopes. It's a Hollywood slow-motion heroes moment if there ever was one.

Jack still seems distracted. My mind has finally changed; I'm starting to get worried now. But the competition re-focuses us. We all concentrate on the task ahead.

All day I'm doing a running TV commentary in my head: *Day One of the UK Inter-Schools Ski Championships. It's the cross-country event! And as with all the events over this three-day meeting at the spectacular slopes of Glenforben, it's against the clock!*

Ten teams, forty competitors, all geared-up for a nail-biting start to this keenly contested under-eighteens competition. The cross-country is a three-mile course of shallow slopes and flat sections, testing strength and endurance to their limits. The course is run four times, ten competitors a time, with one member from each team taking part in each round.

As ever, the favourites are the hugely unlikeable Cargavern High squad. But can the Emerson High team, the defending champions, defy the odds and snatch a second victory from the slavering jaws of the bad guys?

And they're off! Round one is underway, with Emerson High, Cargavern High and a chunky guy from St Something-Or-Other's from Poole, already leading the field.

The chunky guy from St Something-Or-Other's is putting in a good performance, but you can see he's struggling against the steady, measured pace of the Cargavern High man. Emerson High's own Louise Wilder is holding on to second place. She's a rare talent, this girl, the most wonderful combination of beauty, brains and determination to ever walk this earth!

She's edging ahead! She's saved her strength for the final run down to the finish line! The tactic is paying off! The Cargavern High man is WAY behind now!

SHE'S THERE! Round one goes to Emerson High!

BLOODY GENIUS!

Her teammate Allan Snyder hugs her! He's followed by Tom Miller, who hugs her just that little bit longer. And now it's Tom Miller's turn in the next round.

He's nervous as hell! He's lining up with the other competitors. It's a glorious morning here in Glenforben, with sunlight on the slopes and a fresh breeze coming off the mountains. Tom Miller adjusts his goggles and tries to make sure nobody notices how much his left leg seems to be jittering. His heart is POUNDING! HAS he done enough practice? HAS he got the nerve and skill to win this one? CAN he cast his numerous worries about the gorgeous Louise from his mind?

The horn-canister-thing sounds! Miller pulls ahead! Steady on, don't burn out too soon.

The course is a long one. Competitors pass the marker flags at speed.

One's gone the wrong way!

I don't believe it! One dumb twerp has veered off the course!

Dammit! Miller's so busy looking around and laughing at the dumb twerp that Cargavern High have slipped into the lead!

They're passing the spectators' area! Miller is distracted by that alarmingly smart woman in the Emerson High group! Stop shouting encouragement, madam! Miller's HIGHLY embarrassed! He's going to stop and put a ski stick through her chest in a minute!

Into the final slope! There're shouts all around. Miller moves like hell. Neck and neck with Cargavern High.

He's DONE IT! Miller's DONE IT! By a fraction of a millimetre! He records the fastest time this round by fractions of a second.

And it's all going Emerson High's way. Miller hugs Louise Wilder all over again. And then again.

Round Three. Allan Snyder faces that kid from Cargavern High with the line-shaved head. It's a tough call for Miller: he wants to root for his team, but he also wants Snyder to fail miserably and be rejected for ever as Louise's boyfriend of choice.

They're away! And WHAT a showing by a girl from Strasberg Academy in Somerset! She's leading the field. Who is she, by the way? At the halfway point it's Strasberg Academy, Cargavern High, with Emerson High in third place.

But she's peaked! Cargavern and Emerson are pulling ahead! Snyder's on a roll here. He's taken the lead almost half a mile from the finish. Can he keep his position?

YES HE CAN!

It's a clean sweep so far for Emerson High! Who'd have believed it? Snyder has the fastest time of the day, the low-down, wriggling but-admittedly-very-good-on-a-pair-of-skis reptile!

One round left. The shadows of the afternoon are beginning to lengthen. The light is turning a burnt amber as the final ten line up. Among them, Emerson High's own king of comedy, Jack Baker.

It's a VERY quick start! Several of the competitors are determined to make their mark against the two leading schools. The whole field is racing ahead.

But just one mile on, they've spread out considerably. This is what separates winners from losers.

Cargavern High are in the lead by ten metres or more now. Is Baker saving himself for the latter stages?

Apparently not.

Cargavern High ahead by fifteen metres at least. St Something-Or-Other's are second.

What is Baker doing? He's got three competitors right on his heels!

WHAT is going on? There's a sinking feeling in the heart of the Emerson High camp. The other members of the team are watching in silence. Tom Miller is WILLING Baker on, but to no avail!

There's a disaster looming here! Baker is hardly even TRYING. He's PHONING IN his performance!

Cargavern High are DOWN! Miller, Wilder and Snyder are on their feet! Cargavern High have an INJURY! The guy's on the snow! He's pounding the snow with his fist! YES, he's injured! YES! C'mon, Baker!

The remaining competitors are closing in on the finish line, BUT BAKER'S STILL TAKING A WALK IN THE BLOODY

PARK! He barely seems to have NOTICED the chance he's been given!

At the finish, it's St Something-Or-Other's, Strasberg Academy, Emerson High. Baker finishes third.

The day is over, the first event is over, and Emerson High, against the odds, are ahead overall by just under two seconds, thanks to the efforts of the first three team members, and no thanks whatsoever to Team Member Number Four. The competitors return to their hotel, and you don't need a headscarf and a crystal ball to know there's going to be some mixed reactions in the Emerson High camp tonight.

'What the HELL was he playing at!' cries Allan.

We're in my room. I'm propped up against the headboard, Louise is perched at the end of the bed and Allan is pacing about in front of the window. Jack? Dunno.

'Let's get a sense of perspective,' says Louise. 'It's not the end of the world.'

'It could be!' cries Allan.

'It's a game,' I mumble.

'Oi! I am FED UP of that attitude!' cries Allan. 'We've had that too much lately!' He points through the wall, as if he's got Cargavern High on a radar in his finger. 'That lot? On top form? Can wipe the floor with us! They are underperforming! They know it! We know it! We can WIN!'

'We are winning,' says Louise.

'Just!' splutters Allan. 'One more crap turnout by Freak Show and we're finished!'

'Leave him alone,' says Louise. 'There's obviously something bothering him.'

'Too right!' yelps Allan. 'I'll make sure there's something bothering him if he messes this up for us! He wants to pull his act together!'

'Look,' says Louise with a sigh. 'We're all a bit hyper. Why don't we just rest, and get something to eat, and assess things in the morning? Tom, we need that talk.'

'Right.'

Allan flings up his hands. 'Fine. Sure. I'll order Room Service. What do you want?'

'To talk to Tom, alone,' says Louise.

Allan gives her a 'huh?' look. Then he gives me a 'hah!' look. Then he lurches out, whapping the door behind him.

After a long, silent pause I tell Louise about what I saw of Jack last night, and what happened on the plane.

'Now I'm starting to get worried,' she says quietly.

I want to give her another hug, but it doesn't seem appropriate. 'I dunno. Maybe we shouldn't interfere?'

'He wasn't himself today,' says Louise. 'Was he? I mean, he's been in a mood lately, but it's getting a bit beyond that now. Have you talked to him about it today?'

'No.'

'Why not?'

I don't entirely understand the question. I can feel one side of my nose lifting up in an umm-search-me way. 'Dunno. Just haven't. Well . . . not really. Why would I have?'

She shifts slightly on the edge of the bed. 'Because

you're his best friend, that's why. You've known each other since primary school.'

'Well, why don't you go and talk to him, if you think that's what it takes?'

'I've tried that already, haven't I? He doesn't want to talk to me. I've tried to talk to him, Allan's tried to talk to him –'

'What? Allan? When?'

'Weeks ago.'

'It's news to me.'

'Oh shock! That's a surprise! From what went on last night, it's nothing Jack will talk to his parents about either. There's only you. He might talk to you.'

'He didn't on the plane. Why should he now?'

'Why shouldn't he? If you actually talk about what's bothering him, I mean, not about how many superheroes can fit in a phone box!' She stands up and starts walking about. 'Look, we're going around in circles here. The point is, you're his closest friend. Now think, exactly what might have caused this?'

I don't entirely understand the question again. 'I've no idea.'

'Is there something going on at home?'

'I've no idea.'

'Is this competition getting him down for some reason?'

'I've no idea.'

She stops and glares at me. Actually glares. 'Why have you no idea?'

'I just haven't!'

'Is it school? Is he getting behind with anything? Is he feeling pressured by something?'

'I've no idea.'

She lets out an infuriated yelp. I think she may be about to stamp her foot too. 'How can you say that? How can you possibly be the guy's closest friend and have no idea about these things? Doesn't that strike you as . . . cold?'

'No.'

'No.' She snorts angrily, and after glaring at me again goes to stand in front of the window, hands on hips, looking out at the mountains. There is silence, one of those serious silences that wouldn't benefit from even the funniest of funny noises.

She turns to face me again. 'Have you been reading around our current English project?'

'Huh?' I say, pulling a dumbstruck face.

'Remember what I said about reading around the subject? Remember how I said it's where all the useful information is? Have you been reading around ANY subject recently?'

'Errrrrrr, no.'

'Reading around Edgar Allan Poe? Reading around the problems in the lives of Selected Literary Figures?'

'Errrrrrr, no.'

She aims a level gaze at me which pierces my heart. 'It's nothing to be proud of, Tom. You should read Lewis

Wolpert and Elizabeth Wurtzel, and *An Unquiet Mind*, and *The Noonday Demon*.

'Are you saying he's ill?'

'No! I'm saying that if something's bothering him, it should be sorted out. Unresolved issues can have very serious consequences. It's very, very unhealthy to bottle things up.'

'Like after eating a plate of SuperSave fresh pasta!' I say. She looks at me stony-faced. 'Joke,' I splutter.

'How you can sit there and dismiss it like that I just don't know! You are the one and only person who might be able to get through to him, and all you can do is trivialise it! You're so heartless!'

She recoils her way to the door. 'I'm going to try to talk to him one more time, and if he won't, which is more than likely, then all I can do is take my own advice and get some rest and something to eat. Then it's up to you, right? To do something. You.'

If my door gets much more of that whapping when people leave, it's going to come off its hinges. I'm left in the airy quiet of a big room, with thin slivers of my heart littering the floor in a blood-soaked mess.

Heartless? Heartless? That hurts, that really HURTS. And if it hurts so much, I can't be THAT heartless, then, can I? Hah!

I hear Louise's footsteps along the corridor. Then a soft knocking. Then low voices, Louise's in a soft tone, Jack's entirely flat. Then Louise's footsteps again, walking in the opposite direction, back past my room. They don't pause at my door.

I sit there, on the bed, propped up with a pillow either side of me. How long I'm sitting there like that I can't say, because it takes some time for the numbness around my brain to subside.

Tom Miller is heartless. Discuss.

The minutes pass. Or at least, I become aware that the red LED numbers on the alarm clock by the bed are changing.

Louise is right. I am indeed Jack's closest friend, and he has indeed refused to talk to anyone else and it may indeed be that I can make a difference here where others can't. She's right. She's absolutely right. And it wouldn't be interfering.

But, to be brutally honest, I'm nervous.

I'm out of my depth here. I'm not a well-read polymath like Louise. I'm not even a heart-on-my-sleeve shell like Allan.

I'm Prince George, that's who I am.

And how the bloody hell does that help me now?

I'm coming to the firm conclusion that I really need to do that reassessment on myself. But where do I even begin? I'm new to all this.

I can't do this without her. I can't. What am I supposed to say to Jack that isn't on our usual Top Ten Boys Stuff level? I, me, not Prince George, ME?

I leap from the bed, fetch my coat and head for the

corridor. I have to catch up with her. She said she was going to get something to eat, so I'll take her out for dinner. We can discuss approaches to the Jack problem over expensive tomato soup, and then we can come back and talk to Jack together. Yes, that's it! That's it!

We'll go to the place in the village. There's an upmarket inn-type restaurant the teachers from all the various schools went to last night, what was it called? The Niagara, that was it!

I trot along to Louise's room. She's not there. I trot down the wide staircase to where the hotel's dining room and the jaw-droppingly overpriced coffee shop are. She's not there. I trot past Mr Truitt asking at the Reception desk if his suitcase has turned up yet. It hasn't. I trot into Mum in the corridor outside the unisex hairdresser's. She's finishing a phone call, and telling a passing chambermaid to fetch a wet-wipe to that scuff mark on the skirting board over there.

'Mum, have you seen Louise?'

She pops her mobile into her jacket pocket. I don't know how she can use that thing, it's about the size of a pebble. She seems to think anything larger or less obviously expensive is unfeminine. 'I may have some good news for you tomorrow,' she says.

'Great. Have you seen Louise?'

'Don't you want to know what it is?' she says brightly.

'No. Have you seen Louise?'

'Yes, she came past me not two minutes ago. She looked a bit worried. Is everything all right?'

'It will be, Mum, it will be. Where was she going? The swimming pool? The sauna?'

'No, she was on her way out to that restaurant the teachers from all the various schools went to last night, what was it called? The Niagara, that was it. Dreadful wallpaper.'

'What?'

'Awful pattern. Like a 1980s council flat. You'd think teachers would have more taste, but they didn't seem to —'

'No, I mean about Louise!'

'Oh, Allan suggested it, apparently. They went together.'

I return to my bed.

I should have gone to see Jack anyway. I KNOW I should.

But I'm too nervous. I'm too new to this Real Me business. I'm too hurt, and too busy with my own petty jealousies. I don't know what to do, so I do nothing. This new Real Me falls at the first hurdle, gutless and hesitant.

I lie in bed, thinking I'm at the bottom of the barrel, at my lowest ebb, whatever you want to call it, but I know nothing. Compared to the following morning, I'm on Cloud Nine.

In a matter of hours, I will be deeply shocked, twice. After tomorrow morning, life will never quite be the same, ever again.

Chapter 9

I can't sleep. I call for sandwiches and hot chocolate from Room Service at about eleven-thirty, and they're delivered by a waitress who gives me a sideways smile, and curtsies, and calls me 'Your Highness'. I smile back, and thank her very much, and feel obliged to tip her a fiver.

I still can't sleep. But then I close my eyes for a moment, and when I open them there's suddenly grey daylight glowing vaguely around the edges of the curtains.

The red LED numbers on the alarm clock shout 5.11 a.m. I'm wide awake now, so I get up anyway. You can sense it when there's almost nobody else about. The still-ness is so blank and eerie. It makes me feel strangely alone.

I think about going to see Jack. But I still need Louise.

Once I'm washed and dressed I saunter down to the hotel's dining room. Half a dozen staff are bustling about with napkins and silver-plated coffee pots. Normally, sir, we don't begin serving for another half an hour, but I'm sure we can make an exception for you. I smile back, and thank them very much, but there's no way I can afford to start dishing out more fivers. I just smile again, conveying the most intense gratitude in the world, ever, and feeling a bit mean about the fivers.

After tea and toast, and a bit more toast, and scrambled egg, it's still pretty early. I go into Reception. Give it fifteen minutes, and I'll go and wake Louise.

Mr Fenton, the manager, is at the desk again this morning, busy at the screen beneath the counter. I can't take anyone else being pleasant to me, so I take cover in a tall leather armchair with big curling sections at the sides, in which I can't be seen from the desk. I pick up a newspaper from the bulldog-like coffee table in front of me and read about the movie star Mr Fenton mentioned had stayed here last year. Oooh, she's just had a baby. Oooh, she's up for an award. Not for having the baby, I presume . . .

My thoughts are interrupted by Mr Fenton growling at a passing waitress. The cultured lilt of his voice has been barged out of the way by the sound of a ruthless Glaswegian cop from a gritty crime thriller. 'Pola, go check on the cleaners. There's more damned English turning up later and you know what they're like about their lavatories. Live for their bums, they do.'

'OK,' says Pola.

I hear her bustling away to inspect the lavatories, and there's peace and quiet in Reception again, broken only by the occasional tapping of computer keys from Mr Fenton.

And then, two minutes later . . .

My life changes.

I'm reading an article about two musicians on the run from a gangster, which is about as gripping as a greased-up jellyfish, when I hear the glass doors to Reception suddenly heave open. Half a dozen sets of feet clump into the hotel along with a short blast of cold air. I don't take any notice until I hear Mr Fenton bound to attention.

'Good morning, sir!' he says. The Glaswegian cop has gone back to stalking the mean streets.

'Are you the manager? You must be doing a roaring trade while the competition's out of action.'

'I beg your pardon, sir?' says Mr Fenton.

'The Grand! Damn place still isn't open! And I ALWAYS stay there. The stupid jobsworth in charge wouldn't let us in. Not even when *I* spoke to him! Damned "health and safety", or something ridiculous. So we've had to come here.'

I go cold. Seriously.

Because I know that voice.

I've spoken in it, hundreds of times.

'I–I–I don't quite understand, sir,' stammers Mr Fenton. 'Are you saying you're checking out and going to the Grand?'

'Good God, you're as daft as that other one!' exclaims

the real Prince George. There's a chorus of sniggers around him. He starts to speak slowly. 'No. I'm. Checking. In. OK? That's "in", not "out". There's a difference.'

There's a pause. I can barely breathe, let alone move.

'But, sir, your room is still at your disposal,' says Mr Fenton, the voice slipping slightly. 'You, umm, you already have your key.'

I go hot. And then cold again. The key feels like a lead weight in my pocket.

With my paralysed nerves suddenly changing their minds and turning to water, I swivel around in the leather chair. Pulling up my legs, I peep over the top of the chair's back.

That is Prince George. Those must be three of his friends. The two men in suits must be bodyguards.

That is the real Prince George.

The real Prince George leans over the Reception desk. He and his friends are dressed in an assortment of winter outfits bearing the designer labels Massive Expense and Surely Everyone Looks Like This.

'Listen,' says George. 'If I HAD a room key, I wouldn't be wasting my time asking YOU for a room key, now, would I?'

His friends snigger again. Two of them, a boy and a girl, are a living collection of finely chiselled features. The third, another boy, makes Mrs Lovelady look like a supermodel.

'Sir,' says Mr Fenton, smoothing his gelled head in all the places it doesn't need smoothing, 'I don't QUITE understand where our lines are crossing, and so forth, but rest assured that your room is still very much at your disposal. We also have additional premier rooms available for your new guests here, one floor above the rooms of your previous three guests, and additional standard rooms are available for these two gentlemen, sir.' He cocks his head to one side, conspiratorially. 'Would, umm, would these two gentlemen be requiring to be listed as school teachers too, sir?'

'School teachers?' exclaims Prince George loudly. 'Listen, that one there used to shoot terrorists for a living. Dead. Do they look like bloody school teachers?'

'No, sir, no, they look most fearsome and effective, and so forth, sir.'

'Bloody right.'

'Umm, sir, what about the cover story, sir?'

'What? WHAT?' He turns to his friends, who are indulging in yet another giggle. 'Is it me?' he appeals to them. 'Hugo, is it me? Am I the one being peculiar here?'

'It's not you, Pongo,' says the ugly boy. 'Must be a Scottish thing.'

They all laugh. Mr Fenton doesn't.

I do NOT believe it. His friends call him Pongo.

'I sneak away from the bloody press, and bloody meet-and-greets for university courses, to have a few days off with a few chums,' snorts Prince George, 'and I end up in bloody Fairyland! The hotel I ALWAYS use is a bloody building site, and this place looks like it OUGHT to be.' He turns to Mr Fenton. 'Do you realise what time I had to get up this morning? To avoid the bloody press? Do you realise how much pressure I'm under?'

'No, sir, but —'

'No, sir. Now do your bloody job. Hurry along, get our stuff out of the cars, and point me in the direction of the minibar and the peanuts. Chop chop.'

'Yes, sir,' says Mr Fenton. The Glaswegian-cop voice is making a bid for freedom.

I duck back down into the chair. I curl up, not daring to move. I listen to the sounds of hotel staff jumping to it, luggage being fetched and wheeled around, and Hugo noticing the sign which says: *The Hotel Del Coronado welcomes The UK Inter-Schools Ski Championships*. ('We should go along to that, Pongo! Might be a laugh!')

When the main flurry of activity has died down, and all that's left in Reception is a smell of raw cash, I scurry from my hiding place and head for the stairs.

And it's now that it finally hits me. The first of the morning's two shocks.

That was the real Prince George.

If it's possible to stammer as you scurry, then that's what I do at this precise moment. I get a strange feeling that seeps from the pit of my guts and spreads out through my system in horribly biological ways.

I HAVE got it right. I AM absolutely spot on: the stance, the body language, the gestures, the voice, the slightly floppy hair. I have the whole Prince George thing down to the finest detail, and it's all just been confirmed one hundred and ten per cent. Nobody, but nobody, could be Prince George better than me.

Except for one little detail.

He is obnoxious.

Not polite, not charming, not any of the things I have worked so DAMNED HARD on all this time.

Ob – noxious.

It's like running up to whoever is in first place on your Five Most Fanciable Women On TV list, expecting a snog and having her spit in your face instead. It's like having your faithful, beloved pet take a dump on your head in the middle of the night. It's like finishing years of school projects and then watching them burned in your front garden.

I have WORKED on my Prince George persona. I have DEDICATED my looks, my time and my reputation at school to Prince George. I have had Prince George held up to me as an aspirational symbol of niceness and Standards until I'm ready to scream.

And he is obnoxious. He is so far removed from his public image that you'd need a bloody spaceship to reunite them!

What am I doing?

What have I been doing?

What kind of wasted, useless life have I been leading?

I can't be Prince George any more. I can't. I WON'T! I'm NOTHING like THAT.

All those DOUBTS I had about my George-ness, all that

indecision about myself, all those NERVES I've been feeling about . . . What kind of an IDIOT am I?

And what the hell is HE doing now?

I'm at the top of the stairs, looking down the corridor that leads to my room. What WAS my room. His friends' suites are on the next floor, well away from the ones occupied by my friends, but of course 'his' room and 'my' room are one and the same.

The door is open, and growing daylight paints a rectangle across the corridor's decor. Shadows flit back and forth inside the room.

'What's all THIS?' Prince George's voice booms in the stillness. It's still barely breakfast time. My soft-sided suitcase suddenly comes flying out of the room, unzipped sections flapping. It bounces off the opposite wall and collapses to the floor like a carcass. For the time being, I keep my distance.

'They haven't even cleaned this bloody room OUT!' shrieks Prince George. A handful of my clothes flutter into the corridor.

'I think we should trash the place,' says the chiselled girl. 'It'd be SO rock'n'roll.'

'Skis!' exclaims Prince George. 'Someone's left a pair of bloody skis in here!' Out they go.

Hugo whoops with delight. 'Look at this horrible used toothbrush I've found in the bathroom, Pongo!' A second later, my toothbrush ricochets off a light fitting and lands on the carpet.

'Go and get that shabby little manager fired,' says the girl.

'I'm too shattered,' says Prince George. 'I can't be bothered with it.'

'The rest of our rooms are along the corridor and up more stairs,' exclaims Hugo.

The door slams, and their voices are reduced to a low murmur. Hearing movements coming from the nearest rooms now, Allan's and Louise's, I quickly pad along the corridor, pick up all my stuff, prop my skis under my arm and go . . .

. . . Where? I'm not going running to my mum! Apart from anything else I'd have no way to explain things except to tell her the truth. And we can't have that, now, can we?

I can't bunk up with Allan. I won't, on principle. I'm not telling HIM the truth. I'd love to bunk up with Louise, and she already knows what I did, but that's not really possible, is it?

I'll have to share Jack's room. I'll have to tell him the truth, but he'll see the funny side. He won't let on.

Shifting things around a bit, I manage to free a couple of fingers from the awkward bundles I'm holding and tap at his door.

'Jack?' I hiss.

I'm nearly dropping everything. I keep having to bend and wriggle to hold on to it all.

'Jack!'

With my two fingers I twist the handle. The cardboard 'Do Not Disturb' sign falls off on to the carpet. The door swings open and I struggle inside, with my skis clattering against the door frame.

And here's the second shock of the day.

I push the door nearly shut with one foot, and let my stuff fall into an untidy heap. For a second, the thought goes through my head that I'm messing up one of these gorgeous rooms, but the thought vanishes as soon as I look up.

Jack's gorgeous room is a tip. A couple of white towels lie on the floor, looking like I've just caught them mid-crawl as they're making their escape from the en suite. Jack's case is opened and spilled out on a chair. There's a barely-eaten plate of congealed spaghetti bolognaise on the bedside cabinet. The room has a decayed smell to it. Something that's beyond the leftover food. The kind of smell you get in empty waiting rooms.

Jack is curled up in bed, the covers rising and falling slowly as he breathes. They're screwed up around him, in a tight swirl of material. His head lies on a pillow, his face as blank as a fresh sheet of paper.

I'm expecting him to still be asleep, but he's not. His eyes are open, but ringed with fatigue.

'Jack?' I say eventually.

'What?' His eyes blink slowly.

'C'mon. Up and at 'em! Day Two!'

'I'm not going.'

Sounds of people moving about are coming from the corridor. It's breakfast time now. In just over an hour, I must be at the top of a ski slope.

Chapter 10

'Jack?' I repeat. 'Look . . . er . . . What's wrong?' It's pathetic, but it's all I can manage.

The eyes shift focus, as if he's only just noticed I'm here. 'Nothing,' he grunts quietly.

I think about going to fetch Louise, but then I realise that I'm not nervous of this after all. I'm suddenly realising a lot of things. Is it anger that's set me straight? No, not anger: determination. I will be me now. I have wasted my life emulating someone else, but not any more.

I might not be nervous, but I still don't know what to say.

'Hi, Jack. I've . . . er, I've brought all my stuff in here 'cos . . . er, I'm going to need to share your room. Hope that's OK? Yeh? Hey, guess why? Go on, have a guess. You'll never guess.'

'I don't care,' he mumbles.

'Bet you will. You'll laugh, I know you will. The thing is, and this has got to stay between you and me, right? The thing is, the real Prince George has turned up. At this hotel. And, er . . . umm, you see, that's how I got us these rooms. I pretended that I was . . . Are you listening, Jack? It's really funny, right? . . . You've guessed that already, haven't you? Eh?'

'I don't care. Go away.'

'You've got to see the funny side of it! It's one of those Would-You-Believe-It? things, you know, one of those Life-Is-Weirder-Than-Fiction things. Right?'

No answer. He blinks a couple of times. I glance at the clock that's sitting on the bedside cabinet next to the congealed spaghetti. It's eight a.m. Day Two starts at nine.

'C'mon, Jack, you gotta be up! Slalom today! C'mon, we've got to keep that lead!'

'Why?'

'Why? Well, just because! Look, I, er . . .'

I'm floundering. I wish Louise was here.

'Look, I, er . . . I can see there's something . . . I mean, I know there's something wrong. With . . . you, and, er, look, I mean, I just thought that if you wanted to . . . I mean, if there was something that I could do, to, you know . . . ummmmm . . . Help. You.'

'Help?' he says at last.

'Yup,' I say at long last.

'Why?'

He says it like it's final, like there's nothing more that can be said. I struggle to find a way to answer him. My face must look stupid, because I keep forming sentences that don't quite make it into the world of sound.

Jack shifts decisively in his bed. 'I'm not going today. And that's that. I was crap yesterday. Utterly crap. And I'll be crap today. So there's no point.'

'You just had an off day, that's all.'

'Yeh, right. Thanks for the pep talk, but no thanks.'

I wish Louise was here. It's ten past eight.

'Aww, c'mon, Jack. It's not that bad. Sure, I mean, life can suck like a nuclear hoover sometimes, we all know that. But there's no point giving in, is there?'

'I'm not giving in, I'm being realistic. You'll do perfectly well without me.'

'No we won't.'

'I'm not going. I've had enough, OK? It's only a bloody slalom. No more. I haven't slept, I want a rest.'

'And why haven't you been sleeping?'

'No reason. OK?'

Time's getting on. I have to go. Quickly, I gather up all my ski gear.

'Jack? Please?'

No answer. I'm getting nowhere.

'I have to go now,' I say. 'I'll come back later, OK?'

No answer.

There's the sound of movement out in the corridor, and I turn just as Louise appears around the door. She's already kitted up for today's event. She looks at me, then at Jack, then me again. Then Jack again.

'Jack?' she says. 'How are you feeling?'

'Oh, not you as well,' grumbles Jack. He rolls over and pulls the bedclothes over his head.

'At least he let you in here,' whispers Louise. 'That's further than I got with him. I'm glad you changed your mind about helping him.'

'Er . . . right . . . yeh . . .'

Suddenly, we hear voices and bumping from the room next door. Sounds like they're having a peanut-hurling contest.

'Tom, who's that in your room?' says Louise.

Oh dear.

'Cleaners. Must be the cleaners.'

'But it sounds like there's half a dozen of them in there,' says Louise.

'Very efficient staff they've got here.'

'They don't sound like they're cleaning to me,' says Louise suspiciously.

'I told them they could use the minibar,' I blurt. 'You know, as we're getting it free. Come on, we've got to go!'

'I don't think we should leave Jack,' she whispers.

'He's not going anywhere, is he?' I whisper back. 'We need time with him which we simply don't have at the moment. If we scratch the competition, there'll be more than the two of us coming in here wanting answers. Somehow I don't think he'd appreciate that.'

Louise lets out a long sigh. She shuts her eyes for a moment and nods. 'We'll come back and see you soon,' she says to Jack.

He grunts angrily.

Reluctantly, we leave the room. I shut the door behind me quietly, feeling guilty, feeling stupid, feeling I-don't-know-what. I hurry Louise past my (old) room.

Everyone's waiting in Reception. The Cargavern High squad are looking as remote and as brutal as ever, and the St Something-Or-Other's-from-Poole team is getting a motivational talk, delivered by one of their teachers, which is clearly de-motivating them.

Before we can get as far as the Emerson High group, Mr Fenton the manager bounds from behind the desk like a startled gazelle and flags me down. Louise heads for Allan.

'I do hope we can sort out any problems you may be experiencing, and so forth, sir?' he gushes.

'Oh! Yes, yes, everything's fine, thank you.'

In the flash-gaps between the movements of people and ski equipment I can see Louise talking to Allan. He is going ballistic.

'Did you find your key, by the way, sir?' Mr Fenton keeps flattening the extremely flat hair above his ear.

'Sorry? Oh! Yes, I did, thanks.'

Allan is going ape. Louise is stopping him from heading towards Jack's room.

'Because, naturally, sir, we can arrange for another room to be made available to you, sir, if there's still a problem?'

Suddenly, I can't help thinking about how my life has been trashed. I want revenge. 'Mr Fenton,' I say, 'I hope you'll forgive my obnoxious behaviour earlier on.'

'Sir, it's entirely forgotten,' says Mr Fenton, his voice making it absolutely clear that it's about as forgotten as if he'd just written it up in ten metre letters on the hotel walls in his own blood.

'I hadn't taken my medication,' I whisper, in a just-between-you-and-me way.

'Medication, sir?' whispers Mr Fenton.

I nod. Then I put my finger to my lips and hurry away before he can say anything else. I get to Louise and Allan just as Allan is ready to eat one of the leather seats with rage.

'What is he PLAYING AT? Tom! This right? Jack? Not GETTING UP? WHAT is going on?'

'Look, he's, er, not feeling well, and that's all there is to it,' I say.

'Kick up the ass!' cries Allan. 'That's what he wants! Lazy sod!'

'I don't think it's quite that simple,' says Louise quietly.

'Listen to Louise,' I say. 'She's read around this subject.'

'Stuff that!' cries Allan. 'And stuff his attitude! We are THIS close to losing! If we're not one hundred per cent today, that lot over there could wipe the floor with us!'

'He can't compete today!' I say. 'Just accept it.'

'No!' cries Allan. 'We could WIN this! I will NOT have him ruin my chances! I am not going to lose because Mr Happy up there doesn't feel like coming out to play! I am going up to his room! I am going to tell him to pull himself together!'

'You will NOT,' says Louise through gritted teeth.

Allan realises he's losing the fight. He twists on his heels for a moment or two, looking around the crowded Reception area. 'He should lighten up!' he grumbles. 'He should get a grip!'

Louise puts her hands to the side of her head in a wide-eyed Arrrrrgghhh gesture. 'Why did I agree to this again?' she says to herself. 'Why don't I stick to physics? I'm much happier that way.'

There's a sharp clapping of someone's hands from the other side of the leather chairs, and the organisers start today's organising. Mrs Lovelady pushes her way through the crowd, with Mum gliding along in her wake like a freshly groomed cat tripping along behind a warthog it's pretending not to know. She kindly donates a nod of greeting to one or two teachers, and tells a passing chambermaid to fetch a dustpan to those crumbs of food by the plant pot over there. Meanwhile, Mrs Lovelady looks us up and down.

'Where's Baker?' she says.

'He's not well,' says Louise.

'Oh,' says Mum. 'I'll go up and see if there's anything I can do.'

'No,' I say decisively. 'Just a bad cold. He just needs rest.' Instinct tells me that Mum might juuuuuust poooooossibly have Allan's pull-yourself-together attitude to this issue. Allan stands there, simmering.

Normally, it would be much harder than that to stop Mum interfering, but this morning she's looking enormously pleased with herself for some reason. It might be the purple-y outfit she's wearing, which would look fine if she were going to a wedding rather a sports event, or it might be that she's bursting to tell me something. As everyone starts lining up and getting themselves ready to leave the hotel, I can see her choosing her moment. She's bursting to tell me something.

'I can tell you that good news now,' she says.

'What good news?' I say, suspecting very bad news.

'The good news I mentioned last night,' she says. 'I've just got off the phone from the Blue Book agency. It's all confirmed.'

I'm getting a sinking feeling in my gut. 'What's confirmed?'

'Well, I have to admit, it was reading that latest travesty in the *Warwick and District Recorder* on the plane which gave me the idea. There was all that rubbish about you appearing as Prince George while you're up here, but then I thought, "Why not?", so I rang the agency.'

I don't think the feeling in my gut can sink any lower. 'You've . . . booked me a job . . . as Prince George . . . ?'

'Yes, this afternoon, after today's part of the competition. Isn't that good news? We can all go along. It'll be fun. It's at the Grand Hotel, on the other side of the village. They're just finishing a refit, and they're having some big publicity event today. You're a last-minute extra on the programme, apparently. The agency didn't think they could supply anyone, but I happened to phone in, and it's all come together! Isn't that good news? Tom?'

I find myself kind of frozen. There are so many conflicting thoughts going through my head, so many contradictory emotions fighting for my attention that I can barely move. Crushed into my head are Jack, and that twit in my room, and Louise, and the gaping hole where my life used to be, and, and, and . . .

'News? Right. Yeh,' I mumble. No, I can't do it! I WON'T do it! I'm not going to be the public face of Prince Awful any more! Instead, I'm going to be . . . well, I don't quite know yet, the Real Me, somehow, whatever that means, but I'm NOT doing it! Not! Not! Not!

Mum suddenly hugs me. Her mouth pulls into a tight line of suppressed joy, and the vaguest of tears flicker in her eyes. She kisses me on the cheek.

'I'm so proud of you,' she says quietly. 'You'll be brilliant this afternoon, as always. You know, I've been hearing gossip in this hotel all morning that "the real Prince George" is staying here, and how exciting it is. It's wonderful the effect you have on people. Come on, it's time for the competition! Don't worry, you'll do fine! I'll be rooting for you!'

Awww MUUUUUUUM! Don't DO this to me!

I'll have to leave it until later to tell her I'm packing in the Prince George stuff. I can't do it right now.

And how am I going I tell her anyway?

I'm so weak and pathetic.

I can't look Louise or Allan in the face. Everyone's talking as we set off. There's a clatter of skis amongst the competitors and a clatter of thermos flasks amongst the teachers. Mr Truitt pauses at the Reception desk to ask if his suitcase has turned up yet. It hasn't.

UK Inter-Schools Ski Championship, Day Two.

I'm aiming to get things over with as quickly as possible. Here are the main headlines:

1. The weather is glorious, the snow is perfect. It's the slalom event, each team in turn, one competitor at a time.

2. Emerson High are the only team with three competitors. The guy from Cargavern High who fell over yesterday may be even tougher than he looks.

3. The Emerson High team is drawn to go second. Wilder: Two minutes, six point four seconds. Snyder: Two minutes, two point one seconds. Miller: Two minutes, seven point seven seconds. Pretty darn good. Miller is ready to throw a rock at the alarmingly smart woman in the crowd who keeps cheering for him.

4. No other team beats our average, even with four competitors, not even St Something-Or-Other's-from-Poole. Yeehhhh! Except guess-who.

5. Cargavern High go next-to-last. Blistering performance. The kid with the line-shaved head does two minutes dead. The guy who fell over yesterday nearly falls over again, but stays on course and is indeed even tougher than he looks!

6. Final score: Cargavern High take overall lead.

Prospects for Emerson High at the end of the contest tomorrow: now bleak.

I make sure I tell Louise and Allan about Mum's job-booking well before the last of the competitors has done their run and the bleak prospects for tomorrow have started to sink in. I accidentally on purpose forget to tell them that I'm going to tell Mum that I'm packing in the Prince George stuff. It's all getting complicated.

'What about Jack?' says Louise.

'Forget him,' says Allan, not taking his eyes off the Cargavern High team.

'The job's not until this afternoon,' I tell Louise. 'We'll have time to talk to Jack before then.'

'OK.'

I'll also have time to check up on the real Prince George. He and his cronies could be anywhere by now, and be up to anything. It won't take much for the hotel to put two and two together, make er, lemmeesee, four, and have me exposed as the lying fraud that I am.

Hell, there might even be a law against it! Seriously, it's just occurred to me this minute! You get locked up for impersonating a police officer, so you're bound to get more than a wagged finger and a 'Tut tut, don't do it again' for impersonating an heir to the throne!

Why did I do it? WHY?

The last of the competitors passes the finish line. Two minutes, forty-four. Ha ha, rubbish! There's a general air of anticipation about tomorrow and a series of megaphoned proclamations from the organisers.

No need to panic, I think to myself. The job starts at two. There's a clear hour and a half to get back, get changed, monitor the Prince George situation, talk to Jack. Everything is under control.

Mum tugs at my sleeve. 'Come on, the minibus is waiting.'

'Huh?'

'To take us to the Grand. Our hotel are being SO good, I only asked them to book a taxi and the manager said we could use their minibus. He all but insisted. What a nice man.'

'No, Mum . . .'

'What?'

'I've got things that need doing!'

'Like what?'

Yeh, like what? Huh? Huh? What are you going to tell her? 'I've got to go back and, and, and change clothes!' I stutter.

'They've sorted that out too. I said they could go to your room and pick out something smart. The minibus driver will have it all with him.'

'My clothes?' No. HIS clothes! Oh my GOD!

'Come on!' chirrups Mum brightly. 'They're laying on lunch at the Grand.'

'They went to MY room?'

'Yes. You don't mind, do you? They're being SO helpful.'

'There wasn't any, umm, problem?'

'Problem? What DO you mean? The manager's just phoned me to say the minibus is on its way. Come on!'

So George and his cronies can't have been there. They must have gone out. I'm not sure whether that's better or worse.

Right on cue, the hotel minibus squeaks to a stop on the road up ahead. Everyone is trudging back up the slopes, through the snow, chattering and pretending to be really pleased for Cargavern High.

Mum collars Louise and Allan. She entreats all and sundry to come along to the Grand this afternoon. It'll be SUCH fun. She gets a moderately interested response. I am destroyed with embarrassment. I flash Louise a smile that's so weak it needs hospital treatment. She doesn't return it.

Our hotel's barman is once again doubling up as driver of the minibus. He's dabbing the sweat off his head with a greying hanky as Mum and I climb aboard. An expensive suit is draped over one of the back seats, wrapped in cellophane. I think Mum's too excited to notice that this suit is one we couldn't afford in a million, trillion years.

The driver/barman squashes in behind the wheel and the minibus shoots off towards the village of Glenforben. With his neck swivelling like an owl's to keep talking to us, the driver gives us the full story of how he's been to the railway station twice this morning, and he's got to go to some town he's never heard of after he's dropped us off to pick up some business types for some conference at the hotel that's starting tomorrow and he's missed his tea break and he's not going to get a lunch break now, not with these extra trips he keeps having to do, and GET OFF THE ROAD, YOU OLD FOOL!

I keep wondering about Jack.

Chapter 11

'

Where's our Prince George? Oh, you're there! Right. You stand there, then. Don't move. I need to keep tabs on where everyone is. Where's our Tom Cruise?'

The Events Coordinator of the Grand Hotel is called Stanley. I know that because it's stamped in gold embossed letters on his dark blue name badge, which is attached to his sky blue blazer, which is slightly too small for his barrel chest. Underneath his name is printed *Happy To Help You* in letters which are the same shade of off-yellow as his hair.

He's not the only one with a clothing problem. The trousers of Prince George's suit are slightly too short for me. Nobody seems to have noticed, but the air movement around my ankles is getting very irritating.

It's normal for the larger publicity events to book three or four lookalikes. A mix of movie stars and royalty, established icons and people-in-the-news makes for a good press photo, and gives an impression of catering for all tastes. Standing next to me in the huge, low-ceilinged, luxurious banqueting room in which we're gathered are a Madonna and a James Dean. They're staring blankly at Stanley, just as I am. Also, I am trying to ignore the fact that I'm the only one here who's brought an entourage with them, i.e. my mum.

'Are you my Tom Cruise?' says Stanley. There's a hint of helpless dread in his voice.

'No, sir,' says James Dean. 'What time are we finishing? Only, ahh, I gotta be somewhere at six.' (Excellent voice, staying perfectly in character, I'm very impressed.)

'Never mind that,' says Stanley. 'You're not Tom Cruise?'

'No, sir,' says James Dean. (Matchstick in the corner of the mouth, nice detail.)

This news sends Stanley into a panicky flip through the paper on his clipboard. 'But you're Madonna, right?' He points at the other lookalike with a biro.

'Of course I am,' says Madonna in a Welsh accent. She goes back to chewing gum and adjusting her pointy bra. (Just to make it clear, by the way, this is the pop star Madonna, not the religious figure. In case there was any confusion.)

Stanley freezes with indecision for a moment. 'Which agency are you from?' he gasps at James Dean.

'Logan, Axelrod and Rubin, my friend,' says James Dean.

'Right,' he declares through gritted teeth. He walks away across the wide expanse of thickly sound-deadening carpet. A few minutes later, he returns.

'They say they sent me a Tom Cruise,' he sighs. 'But you're not Tom Cruise.'

'No, sir,' says James Dean.

'Who are you then?'

He suddenly drops out of character. 'I'm James Dean! Who do you bloody think? God almighty!'

'Where's the stage?' says Madonna. 'You haven't said how many numbers you want me to sing.'

'None!' gasps Stanley. 'I don't want any singing!'

'But I'm a singing Madonna,' says Madonna. 'I've done cruise ships and everything. I do the whole package.'

'I'm not paying for singing!'

'You are now I'm here!' exclaims Madonna. 'I'm not coming all this way for nothing!'

James Dean starts wandering about.

'Please,' says Stanley urgently. 'Stay put. I need you to stay put, please. Right here. I can't get things straight if you're not here. Please. Thank you.'

He hurries away again.

'Well, this is a right cock-up, innit?' mutters Madonna. James Dean starts wandering about again. Soon they've both disappeared down the passageway which leads to the patio at the back of the building.

I'm starting to get impatient. It's nothing to do with Stanley, or the Grand, or Madonna. Well, actually, it IS, but it's mostly to do with the fact that I'm standing here, in a (stolen!) suit, waiting for a crowd of press and public to turn up and gaze at me like I'm in a ZOO! It's to do with the fact that I'm carrying on with this trivial rubbish while Jack Baker is over on the other side of the village so preoccupied with something that he's not himself any more. It's to do with the fact that I'm FED UP with a certain royal person. It's to do with the fact that it's time I ditched this kind of meaningless crap HOWEVER much it pays, and HOWEVER many passive-aggressive guilt-trips get heaped on me by my MOTHER!

It's to do with the fact that if I'm going to be me, and not someone else, it's time I bloody well STOOD UP FOR MYSELF, STOPPED BEING A HUMAN DOORMAT AND MADE A FEW DECISIONS!

Mum is standing by the high window at the far side of the enormous room, flipping through the Grand's brand new sales brochure and admiring the view across the patio.

Stanley reappears, clutching a fresh wad of paper. 'Where the hell have the other two gone?' he cries suddenly.

'Excuse me, I can see them from here,' calls Mum politely from the corner. 'They're out on the patio.'

I'm getting REALLY cheesed off.

'Right, they're fired!' says Stanley. 'That's unprofessional. I told them to stay here. They're both fired! Not you, Prince George. You're not fired. You're cutting the ribbon! Stay put! No, please, I mean it! I can't get things done if you're running around the hotel unsupervised! I need you in TWO MINUTES!'

I'm marching over to where Mum's standing.

I've had it.

That's it.

No more. I'm me now. Whoever that is.

Mum pulls a stretchy-mouth face at me as I approach. 'It's not very well organised, is it? Never mind, you'll be the star of the show now.'

'There won't be a show, Mum. I've made up my mind.'

'Sorry?'

'I'm packing it in. The whole lookalike business. The whole Prince George thing.'

'Oh, I know this is a bit of a shambles, but there's no need to get upset about it.'

'I'm not "upset", Mum,' I say, with an icy calm which impresses even me. 'I am giving it up. As of now. It's all a big fat lie.'

'Tom! This isn't you,' says Mum with a frown.

'So who is it, Mum? Hmm? Who am I?'

Her frown gets deeper. 'What ARE you talking about?'

'Exactly. I'm sorry, Mum, I don't mean to cause any-body any grief, I really don't. But enough's enough. I am not Prince George, and Prince George is not me. Believe me, I know.'

'What's the matter, Tom? You're being silly.'

'No, Mum, I'm being normal.'

I march for the big double doors that lead into the room. As dramatic exits go, it's looking good. Mum skips over to Stanley. As I bump the doors open and march through, I hear them talking in lowered, urgent voices.

Oh.

I'm in the kitchens. Not such a good dramatic exit after all: I've gone through the wrong doors.

There's nobody in here. Stanley said that the Grand wasn't reopening for business for another couple of days, and that this afternoon's event is simply timed to hit the papers at the right moment. So for now, the kitchens are an echoing vault of white tiles and polished chrome surfaces.

I haul myself up on to one of the worktops and sit there. I'm feeling . . . I really haven't got the faintest idea what I'm feeling.

I can't go back out there. It'll ruin my dramatic exit. I'll have to wait a while. Sneak out the back way, maybe. Go and sit in the minibus, if it's back yet.

Whether I'm sitting there brooding for any length of time, I don't know, because I'm so wrapped up in wondering what to do next. But the next thing I'm aware of is the sound of people, coming from the banqueting suite I've just left. Quite a large number of people.

Ah. My public awaits. Well, they can await me all they like.

And it's just as this tiny little morsel of defiance runs through my head that I catch sight of one of Prince George's menacingly tailored bodyguards, standing at the back of the kitchen, looking like a business executive on steroids. He's ditched the dark glasses. Even so, he hasn't spotted me.

My throat skips a beat, or my heart gets a lump in it, I don't know what, I'm so startled. I'm ducked down behind a huge, sleek steel cooker before the bodyguard's even taken a step.

He walks right through the kitchen, shiny shoes clacking on the tiles, and gives a short whistle as he nears the doors I just came through. Sure enough, Prince George and his chiselled friends troop through, ugly Hugo and the other bodyguard bringing up the rear. The chiselled friends are smirking amongst themselves.

'I love this sort of thing,' says Prince George. 'Makes me feel like a spy.'

'Good thing they didn't swipe your dinner jacket,' says the chiselled girl. 'You can't look like a proper spy without your dinner jacket.'

Prince George motions to the bodyguard nearest the doors. 'Go and find the person in charge. I don't care what they told me this morning, they can bloody well put me up whether the place is open or not. I've stayed at Balmoral, I'm used to slumming it.'

'Sir,' says the bodyguard. In his voice I think I detect a hint of why-oh-why-didn't-I-transfer-to-CID-while-I-had-the-chance.

The bodyguard swings the double doors open, and they stay rocked back on their hinges. There's an enthusiastic round of applause. There are about a hundred people standing in the banqueting hall.

'Who the bloody hell are these people?' says Prince George quietly.

Both bodyguards skip ahead of him. They don't know who the bloody hell these people are either.

Photo-flashes sparkle here and there. There's another enthusiastic round of applause. Allan is standing over to one side. My mum is beside him.

Prince George waves at them all. For the instant that follows – JUST for that one instant – I find I have to admire the guy. He's assessed the situation, and his mask is raised. He's that ever-so-nice, man-of-the-world prince now, the one in the papers, the one on TV.

Except that this crowd think he's me. Pretending to be him. They think they're seeing a lookalike.

'Oooh, he's not so tall in real life, is he?' says a voice from the crowd.

'Hellooo, Prince George! Prince George!'

'Rubbish! Looks nothing like him!'

Him, me, me, him, them, it's all an insane crush in the head for a minute or two. But only for a minute or two, because after some more waves and hand shaking Prince George starts whispering to his bodyguards and they start herding people out of the room. Stanley, who's been hovering nervously around the press corps, starts getting indignant.

'Oi!' He pokes the nearest bodyguard on the shoulder. 'He's got to cut the ribbon yet! I haven't done the ribbon!'

'Are you in charge here, sir?' says the bodyguard.,

'Yes I am!' yelps Stanley. 'Where did you extra people come from? I'm not paying for extras. You two guard people look quite good, but who are you three?' He jabs a finger at George's friends. 'Who are you supposed to be? Are you friends of the boy's mum?'

'Well, I've met her a few times,' says Hugo, looking slightly confused.

The bodyguards are efficiently clearing the room. Stanley is inefficiently trying to stop them.

'Oi! No! I'm not having just two minutes! I paid to have him until four o'clock! We haven't done the ribbon yet! Oi!'

The bodyguards ignore him. Two very tall men from the press step forward and attempt to introduce themselves to Prince George.

'Jim Dougherty,' says the one in the spotless, dark blue double-breasted suit. '*Glenforben Advertiser*. Johnny Hyde.' He indicates the other one, in the spotless, light grey double-breasted suit. 'Photographer. Can we have a word? Short interview? Won't take a moment?'

Johnny Hyde says nothing. He holds his whopping great camera against his chest like a shield.

The bodyguards move swiftly to intercept the pair of them. 'Sorry, sir, interviews have to be agreed in advance!'

Jim Dougherty thinks it's all part of the act. He stands with pen poised over notebook. 'Love these heavies! Nice touch! So, what's your name, son?'

Prince George stares blankly at him.

'Have you done this sort of thing much before? What do your friends think about you being Prince George?'

Prince George stares blankly at him.

I catch sight of Allan's face. He is thoroughly enjoying himself. I catch sight of Mum's face. She is totally entranced.

The bodyguards are getting very jittery. Two of them aren't enough to round up the crowd and shepherd them away from Prince George. Most of the press and locals are doing as they're told, assuming the brief show is over and that it wasn't up to much, but some are meandering around the guards and spreading out across the breadth of the banqueting hall. The other lookalikes appear from behind the crowd, both of them now changed back into their regular clothes.

Allan is heading out with the rest of the crowd. He is hugely impressed with the bodyguards.

My mum is still totally entranced. She is standing completely still. Her expression of confusion is the stillest thing about her, but there are pages of information scrolling across her face.

She's wondering where the bodyguards came from. She's wondering who 'my' three friends are. She's wondering why 'I' appear to be slightly shorter in the leg. I think she may have finally noticed that the clothes 'I' am wearing are not mine. (He's in a tweedy-looking jacket and black trousers). She's very, very confused.

She thinks this should be me, but she realises there's

something wrong here, that it isn't me, but surely it must be, but it isn't, but . . . Fair enough, you don't expect to see your lookalike son suddenly replaced by a real heir to the throne, do you? Fair enough. You don't expect a royal to suddenly appear through a kitchen door, do you? Can't argue with that.

But EVEN SO! I'm finding it positively upsetting that she's genuinely confused. Just HOW submerged in Prince Awful have I been?

The men from the *Glenforben Advertiser* are being man-handled out of sight by the guards. Jim Dougherty is laughing to himself and shouting questions at Prince George.

Allan has gone, as have the rest of the crowd by now. The other lookalikes are milling about, waiting to vent their frustrations on Stanley. Stanley is venting his frustration on Prince George.

'What a shambles!' he shouts. 'Who do those two thugs think they are? Who do YOU think you are!'

And now, every member of the press has left the room. Prince George can take the mask off. 'I beg your pardon?' he says to Stanley, very slowly.

'If you think I'm paying you ANYTHING, you're in for a shock! I am not paying you. I am not,' says Stanley.

Prince George detonates. 'Will somebody tell me WHAT THE BLOODY HELL is going on here? Who the HELL authorised a press call? WHO?'

'Tom!' cries Mum, skittering over to Prince George.

'Really!' She's still not at all sure who she's talking to, you can tell. But cold logic is winning out over gut feeling here, and cold logic is telling her that the idea of her son being mysteriously replaced by the real royal he's an exact lookalike for is totally absurd. Frankly, I'm feeling hurt!

'Who are you?' says Prince George.

'Tom! What's got into you today?' says Mum.

'Stop calling me that!'

The guards march over, having seen the last of the stragglers out. 'Is this lady bothering you, sir?' says one of them.

'She certainly is, throw her out,' says Prince George.

The bodyguards get hold of her arms and begin to drag her away. Mum lets out a gasping squeal of indignation. 'Do you mind! This is my son!' She shrugs herself free.

Prince George's friends burst out laughing.

'Oh GOD!' says Prince George. 'Another loony.' He pats Mum on the head. 'Yeeees, madam, you're my mother, madam, now run along to whatever institution has let you out for the day. I'm sure they'll be missing you around the ping-pong table.'

His friends fall about laughing.

'Tom!' gasps Mum. She's torn between anger and tears. 'Where did these two men come from? I want to know what's going on.'

'What's going on?' says Prince George. 'I come here, on the quiet, to get away from the doddering crumblies at Windsor Museum, and I'm surrounded by loonies. Do you think it's something in the water, chaps?'

His friends supply him with an assortment of search-me expressions. Hugo starts looking Mum up and down.

'She's very smart for a loony,' he says. 'Don't they usually have carrier bags or something?'

'Do you have a carrier bag, madam?' says Prince George. Mum looks like she's about to throw him over her knee and give him a smacked bum.

And then her face is instantly wiped clean. She twigs that the totally absurd really has happened, that she should have trusted gut feeling all along. Now her expression keeps shifting back and forth between alarm and horror.

Back and forth, back and forth.

'Fabulous,' says James Dean. The lookalikes have gathered behind Mum and are staring closely at Prince George as if he's being exhibited in a glass case. 'That's the sign of a true professional,' he says. 'Not breaking character for one minute. Brilliant.'

'Naaaah,' says Madonna. 'The look's OK, but he's nothing like the real thing, is he? Grumpy little so-and-so.'

'Oh, I don't know,' says James Dean. 'I bet they're all stuck-up like that when they're not putting on a show for the proles.'

'Are you addressing ME?' says Prince George. He swings around to his friends. 'Which is the maddest, do you reckon? This hotel or the Del Colostomy, or whatever it's called?'

'Too close to call, Pongo,' says Hugo, laughing.

Prince George swings back to the others. 'Do you know

why I came along here this afternoon? I'll tell you, shall I? At the Del Colostomy I had a suit stolen from my room. Not by some character in a mask and a stripy shirt, mind you. No, no, no, by the staff. We get back from doing a bit of shopping, and that oily little tick of a manager says to me he's put my suit in a minibus. So here I am again, back at the Grand, and THIS place has turned as bloody weird as the other!'

Mum's voice is slightly chipped at the edges. 'Y–Y–Your . . . Highness?' she says at last.

'Ding!' shouts Prince George. 'Bingo! The penny's dropped! Not a loony after all!' He speaks at her in a raised voice, as if she's pretending to be deaf and he's pretending to humour her. 'Are you with the hotel, dear? Are we back in the land of the sane? Two knocks for yes, one knock for no. Run along and get us some lunch. I'm bloody famished.'

His friends cackle. Mum takes a step backwards. Actually, more like a stagger backwards.

Her voice is chipped in multiple places. 'How dare you speak to me like that,' she says quietly. 'You . . . rude . . . arrogant . . . nasty little boy!'

With a derisive sniff, she pulls herself up to her full height, tugs at the hem of her jacket to straighten it, turns on her heels and walks out.

'Bye bye,' says Prince George. His friends giggle.

The lookalikes saunter away. 'Quite amazing,' says James Dean. 'Even his mum plays along with it. You've got to take your hat off to the pair of them. Brilliant.'

Stanley is fighting back the tears. 'I can't take any more today. I can't. Goodness knows what coverage we're going to get now, if any. I've just had it with the lot of you! I hate you all!'

He flings his clipboard to the carpet. It bounces harmlessly. Sheets of paper flutter off it as he runs for privacy.

Prince George is left standing in the middle of the room, his bodyguards on one side and his bemused friends on the other.

'Mad,' he says, in the sudden stillness of the room. 'They're all bloody mad.'

Chapter 12

Later, back at the Del Coronado, I've taken cover in the hotel's jaw-droppingly overpriced gift shop with Louise. We're pretending to be fascinated by a display of souvenir kilts, and T-shirts with *Hotel Del Coronado, Glenforben* on them. I give her the money to get me a tartan baseball cap and pull it low over my face in case the hotel manager spots me and I get dragged into another awkward conversation.

Louise brings me up to speed on what she did after I'd departed from the ski slopes in the minibus, heading for the Grand: first, she comes back to the hotel and once the competition formalities of the day are completed she heads straight for Jack's room.

She takes him a sandwich, which he doesn't touch. She sits with him for a while but gets very little out of him. She goes to the hotel's internet terminals and does some more reading around the subject, then heads for Reception and waits for me to get back.

Allan passes through a couple of minutes later, tells her how cool I looked with bodyguards and a posse, and says he never appreciated how sharp my lookalike image could be. Then my mum passes through, without appearing to notice anyone or anything.

As we head back to Jack's room, I bring Louise up to speed on what I did after everyone had left the Grand: I get noticed by Prince George's bodyguards and hauled out in front of him. The experience is disturbingly mirror-like.

Once Prince George's friends have stopped pointing and howling with laughter at me, and once he's had the full story of what I'm doing here, he spends a few minutes making it crystal clear what he thinks about lookalikes, ending with the words '. . . bunch of irresponsible, thoughtless, parasitic leeches'.

'Well,' I say, 'it's not my fault if I look like you. Or is it that you look like me?'

'Oh, don't give me that old bilge, I've heard it all before. Dress down, comb your hair the other way, and you can go unnoticed. Am I right? Yes, I know I am. You can turn it on and off at will. Well, I can't.'

'How awful for you,' I say, 'being born into vast wealth, automatic respect, international influence —'

'Influence? Me? I only have to say I like the beach at Cannes and I've got the English Tourist Board practically yelling "traitor" at me! What opinions can I ever express, eh?'

'Good thing too,' I grumble. 'You're so rude.'

'Listen, you ignorant little troll, being rude to people with no comeback is one of the few pleasures I get in life! People like you, who live off my image like publicity tape-worms, get all the best bits and none of the hassle. I bet you get girls swarming around you at your inner city compre-hensive, don't you? Eh?'

'. . . No.'

'Yes, you do! And do you think I get any of that? Any girl I so much as glance at gets dragged through the gossip columns for six months. Decent totty runs a mile from me.'

'I wonder why,' I mumble. 'At least you're still —'

'What? Rich? Powerful? Listen, Tommy-whoever-you-are, I don't just have a job, I AM my job. I didn't choose it, and I can't leave it. I can't even SIGN MY NAME on most things, did you know that?'

'Actually, yes, I did –'

'Oh, go away!' He wags a few fingers at me dismissively. 'You're boring me now. Come on, chaps, we're off. Leave the stuff in the cars, we're going to Cannes, for the beach. Stuff the English Tourist Board, I'm fed up with this madhouse.'

And off they went.

'Did you know he was coming here?' says Louise in a low voice.

'No, I swear!'

'And he really can't get a girlfriend?'

'No, I swear!'

'Did your mum get to see him?'

'Yes. Yes she did.'

'I suppose she's floating in a state of bliss now, then?'

'Er, possibly, possibly. Put it this way, I think that from now on, she's going to make sure I wring every last penny out of my Prince George lookalike jobs.'

'Why do you say that?' she says. She's looking slightly deflated.

'Well, she'll be very keen for me to uphold Standards. They've, er, slipped recently, and she'll be wanting me to return them to their former high level. Believe me, I know her, and if there's one thing she's going to be even more dedicated to from now on, it's maintaining the Stiff Upper Lip of the British Royal Family. She can ignore any quantity of bad news on that score, I assure you.' I think uncomfortable thoughts for a few moments. 'Although, she is also going to kill me.'

'Why?'

'Because I've told her I'm packing the whole thing in.'

'Packing it in?' she says brightly. She stops looking slightly deflated and starts looking very attentive instead.

'Yes. I've decided. It's time to be me. That's it. I've made up my mind. I'm not doing it any more.'

'Really?' she says.

'Really really,' I say.

She looks at me a bit funny. At the time, I take very little notice of that funny look, what with all the slush that's sloshing about in my mind, but that funny look has enormous significance.

'Mum is going to kill me,' I say.

By now, we're back at Jack's room. He's asleep and the room is still a tip. Louise opens the window slightly, to let in some fresh air. It's distinctly cold outside.

'This suit is surprisingly warm,' I say. My voice sounds far too loud, even though it's next door to a whisper.

We let Jack sleep. We presume he needs it. We each pull up one of the armchairs and slump down to wait, not entirely sure if there's anything else we should be doing. Louise makes a quick call to her mum back home, and then we get some outrageously high-calorie filled baguettes from Room Service, because we're both tired and want comfort food. It's pitch black outside and the only light in the room is the diffused glow from the bedside lamp.

'These chairs are comfy, aren't they?' I say and don't even realise I'm dropping off to sleep.

When I wake up, very slowly, the dreams I've been having vapourise like bathroom mist. I can feel them slipping out of reach. I don't want them to, but I don't know why because by now I can't remember what they were about.

As my consciousness returns, the weight of reality gradually becomes apparent again. I glimpse where I am and why. I discover I'm curled up in my armchair, feet poking over one side, elbows flopped around my face.

The bedside clock says it's five in the morning. I wriggle around to sit upright, rubbing the back of my hand against my face. I'm wide awake now. My breathing sounds noisy in the silence.

Louise is still out cold. She's sitting, legs sticking out, arms folded, with her head resting on the arm of her chair. Her mouth is slightly open. I think she's been dribbling. Somehow it makes her look all the more cute.

She is beautiful. It suddenly occurs to me that I've never seen her asleep before. Her features are so perfectly set. She looks very young and very adult, all at the same time.

I love her. And she doesn't love me.

She makes a sudden piggy snort and jerks awake as if someone's prodded her with a broom handle. She blinks a few times and scratches at the corner of her eye.

'Y'OK?' she mutters.

'I've just woken up too,' I say.

'What about you?' she says.

She's talking to Jack. I have to twist slightly to see his face, deep in the bed covers. He's wide awake as well. How long's he been awake? He glances at Louise as if he can't understand why anyone would ask him such a question.

'What you two here for?' he mutters.

Louise shoots me a glance which declares 'Over to you' in no uncertain terms.

Over to me.

'Er, look, we, umm, we just want to help,' I say, clearing my throat a couple of times to shake off the night.

'I'm going to go and wash,' says Louise. She heads for the en suite. I don't know whether this is a strategic withdrawal, so I can do what I'm supposed to do and get Jack to talk, or whether it's just a girly-clean thing. Either way, I wish she'd stay with me. With us. No, just with me, really.

I hear the ka-cling of the bathroom light being pulled on, and a soft, thin bar of light appears beneath the door.

I change seats, so I'm facing Jack. Louise's chair is still warm.

'How . . . er, how are you?' I say, eventually.

Jack breathes in and out a couple of times. 'Does it matter?'

'Yeh, course it matters.'

Long embarrassing silence.

'Louise has told you to come and talk to me, has she?' says Jack.

'Nooooo! . . . OK, yes. She's getting worried. We're both getting worried.'

'Why can't you just let it go?'

'Well, because YOU'RE not letting it go, are you? Whatever it is that's bothering you.'

Long embarrassing silence.

I have a feeling that the Real Me is struggling to emerge here, somehow, some way or other, but I'm still having trouble with the thickness of my protective coating of Prince George. Eventually, I let out a long sigh.

'There'll be a hell of a fuss if we're not in the competition today,' I say.

'You're not going to talk me round, OK? Forget the stupid competition. It's absolutely irrelevant, and my taking part in it is the most irrelevant thing about it.'

'But we might win.'

'But we probably won't.'

'But we might.'

'But we won't.'

'So you're throwing in the towel, then?' I say. 'You're just giving up because it's difficult?'

'I'm giving up because it's beyond my ability to change!' cries Jack angrily. 'See sense, will you?'

My voice is rising. 'There! That's it, right there! That's why I won't let it go. That's not Normal-Jack talking. Jack Baker does not quit at the first level boss. Jack Baker does not give up like that. You're the one who's been pulling us through since Miss Annabel Norris left. You're Jack Baker, Emerson High's King Of Comedy. All of this . . .' I sweep my arms around to indicate Jack's dishevelled appearance, Jack's dishevelled bed and Jack's dishevelled room. 'This isn't You. This is not You. And it makes me worry about . . . you . . .'

Long embarrassing silence.

'Look,' I say, almost before I know I'm saying it. 'Stick me in a pink dress and call me a girly, but I'd rather like to have Normal-Jack back again, OK? There!'

I swear I can suddenly feel make-up on my face and high heels on my feet. Or is it just crawling emotional discomfort?

Eventually, my voice emerges again, deliberately softer. And deliberately at a lower pitch.

'Can you see my point, Jack? I'm bound to get worried, aren't I? Normal-Jack is a self-assured guy.'

He gives out a mirthless snort of hilarity and avoids my gaze. 'I'm glad you think so.'

'But you are.'

'No, I'm not.'

'That's just low spirits talking.'

'No, it ISN'T.' He's REALLY avoiding my gaze now. 'A genuinely self-assured guy would have a certain composure, wouldn't he? He would NOT have to cultivate an air of amused indifference. Like I do. Or swan around the edges of every social circle looking deliberately detached. Like I do. Right? Believe me, I've thought about this a LOT. So am I actually self-assured? Is that a true picture of me? Is that this Normal-Jack character you're on about? I'm glad you think so, because I sure as hell don't. If you think I'm really like that, underneath it all, then that just proves what a good job I've done. It's all a front.'

'But,' I splutter, 'why have you never said any of this before?'

I think to myself: *Stupid bloody question! Why did I hide behind Prince George? Why can't I tell Louise how I feel? Why didn't I ask Jack about Louise that day in the canteen? And so on, and so on, spiralling down to the basic DNA of the human male . . .*

'But,' I splutter again. 'But your accent thing, with all the teachers. That takes real guts, real talent!'

'It's just showing off. It's attention-seeking. It's childish.'

'But what about your stand-up act? Oh, come ON, that's brilliant! You CAN'T say that's not a unique piece of Normal-Jack!'

He sighs. He's staring straight up at the ceiling. The bedclothes are pulled up tight around him.

'I dunno,' he whispers at last. 'I suppose so. But it seems so silly and vacuous now, though.'

Silence.

'But why?' I say. 'What's happened?'

Long silence.

Long, long silence.

'My mum left home,' he says quietly. 'Middle of last holidays. Left a note and went.'

'Jack, I —'

'I don't mind. Not really. It's not like it wasn't long overdue. The house is nice and quiet. No explosions, no guilt trips. Makes a change.'

'Even so, no wonder you're preoccupied.'

He snorts a non-laugh. 'Oh, that's not the half of it. You know why she left? You know what finally pushed her over the edge? My dad's financial chickens have come home to roost. Shady business practices, tax dodges, they've all gone belly up. Somebody, somewhere, cross-referenced something, and now the Revenue and Customs are after him. He got a letter. Hand-delivered, no less, and full of phrases like "under investigation" and "serious legal consequences". Then nothing, for weeks. While they investigated. You know, I never appreciated the true meaning of "unbearable tension" before. Mum had a screaming fit, and the next day she was gone. Dad started collecting accountants for a hobby. We're going to lose our house, and everything in it. Dad will be lucky to avoid criminal charges.'

'Bloody hell . . .' I whisper.

'I thought, hell, I can cope. It's all their fault. It's all down to their own selfish stupidity. Nothing to do with me. But I can't switch it off. I saw a movie the other week, some suspected crook in a brightly lit room with a tape recorder and two cops with necks thicker than their heads. "Just following standard procedure, sah!" And it frightened the living hell out of me.'

'Oh, come on, nothing like that's going to happen to you!'

'But what if it does? I don't know! What does "under investigation" MEAN? Am I going to get dragged into this? I jump out of my skin every time the doorbell rings. Every time I see someone official-looking walk past the house my guts turn inside out. I'm scared to look at what arrives in the post. It's like there's something poisonous running round and round inside my head, and I can't get it out.'

Long silence. Jack looks grey.

I almost jump out of my skin myself when I realise that Louise is silhouetted in the bathroom doorway.

How long has she been standing there? How much of all that did she hear?

As she steps forward, she swipes at her cheek with the back of her hand. Most of her is still in shadow. She sits in the other armchair, and puts a hand on to the thick, wrinkled-up hotel counterpane that covers Jack's bed.

'Jack?' she says. The voice of an angel.

'Yeh?'

'However bad the problem is, it can be sorted out.'

He eyes her guardedly. Discomfort oozes from all over him.

'I can understand how awkward this is for you,' she says. 'But you've nothing to be ashamed of. You've got to face the fact that you're going to have a very tough time until all this is dealt with.'

I lean over to her. 'Er, shouldn't we sugar-coat this a bit?' I say in a stage whisper.

'No, we shouldn't,' she says, looking straight at Jack. 'Jack's an intelligent guy. He can face up to it. I know he can; I've got every faith in him. But he mustn't bottle it up any more. Unresolved issues and buried emotions can come back at you in some pretty horrible ways.'

'Listen to her, Jack,' I say. 'She's been reading around the subject.'

Jack is quiet for a long time. Her hand never moves from him.

'One thing's for sure,' she says quietly. 'This is way, WAY out of our league. I seriously doubt things are as bleak as you fear, and I'm so glad you've told us what's wrong, but you need to talk to someone who can give you some practical help. Which we can't. Before we all go home, why don't you talk to Mrs Lovelady?'

'Really?' I say, wrinkling a nostril.

Louise's eyes don't move off Jack. 'Sure. Remember Big Henry's broken leg? She'd take it seriously, I know she would. We can't deal with this ourselves.'

She sits back in the armchair. She runs a hand across her forehead.

'We've got to get ready soon,' she says. 'Last day today, the downhill.'

'Will you come with us, Jack?' I say. 'We've got to be blistering today, or Cargavern are going to slaughter us. How about it?'

He visibly shrinks. 'No, I can't. I'll be crap.'

'Please, Jack?' says Louise. 'Can you just come and watch, maybe?'

'. . . No . . .'

'Aww, c'mon,' I say, 'where's Normal-Jack's get-up-and-go?'

'I told you,' says Jack, 'it doesn't exist.'

'Well, it exists as far as I'm concerned. You had everyone fooled. Look, if all that Jack-ness of yours was just a front, well then, so what? I say, if you can LOOK it, you can BE it. Believe me, with everything that's happened lately, I know!'

'Oh yeh, that's easy for you to say, Golden Boy!' There's a real bitterness in his voice.

'What's that supposed to mean?' I say.

'When are you ever going to be short on something like that?' he says. 'Or a future? All you have to do is turn into Prince Charming, and everything's right there for you. Girls, attention, money, fame. One look at you, and everyone's your best mate.'

'But I'm giving it up! Louise, tell him, I'm giving it all up!'

'Yeh, right,' growls Jack.

I jump to my feet.

The idea hits me like a brick between the eyes.

'Wait there!' I cry. 'Sorry, stupid thing to say! Just . . . wait there!'

I head for the corridor.

'Tom?' calls Louise.

'Back soon!' I shout, already out of the room and running.

Brilliant idea! I race down the wide staircase into the even wider area that leads to Reception. This idea is so darn cool I can hardly stop myself giggling with glee.

Cut to: me, downstairs, sitting in that hairdresser's chair. Cut to: forty-five minutes later, back at Jack's room. I walk into the room and stand there, arms wide, silently asking for comments.

'What the hell have you done?' mutters Jack.

Louise's lips curl, to stop a laugh escaping. 'Wow,' she says eventually.

'Whaddya think?' I say.

My new hairstyle is radical, to say the least. It's very short, it's very spiky, and it alters my whole look. It's dyed much lighter, too. If someone came up to me now and I said to them, 'I worked as a Prince George lookalike', they'd wrinkle the corners of their mouths and think, 'In your dreams, sunshine.'

'Well?' I say.

'I think it suits you,' says Louise, with a grin.

'I went down to the hotel hairdresser's,' I say, as if it wasn't blindingly obvious.

'Why?' says Jack.

'Well, lots of reasons. I've been thinking a lot recently. You know, getting my priorities straight,' I say. 'I told you, I'm finishing with the whole Prince George business, for good. And there's no going back now, not with this haircut! I'm throwing myself into space here. I'm jumping off the high wire without looking to see if there's a net. YOU'VE got to take a leap, so I'VE taken a leap. There! Now, if I can do it, so can you!'

His eyes narrow a little. 'Is that a wig?'

'No, of course it's not a wig!' I cry. I pull at my cropped spikes. 'Yeeek, there's hardly anything left of my hair, is there?'

Jack blinks a couple of times.

'We gotta go!' I declare. 'Wilder, to your room! Prepare to kick Cargavern butt!'

She salutes. 'Aye aye.'

'Baker! We're off to get changed. I'm off to have a quick bath, because I'm sure that hairdresser could smell me. You . . . ahh . . . you come along if you can. Just come and cheer us on, yeh? We'll be rootin' for ya!'

I hustle Louise out of the room. As we hurry back to our rooms, I pull a helpless face at her.

'It was all I could think of,' I whisper. 'I didn't know what else I could do.'

She grins at me.

Chapter 13

Day Three.

The Emerson High party are huddled to one end of the spectators' area. The air is sharply cold again today, despite the dazzling sunshine, brighter than ever before.

Mrs Lovelady is guzzling hot soup from her thermos, and not giving Mr Truitt any. Mr Truitt is shivering in his thin brown suit. He's been wearing it for four days now.

Mum's beside them. I haven't had a chance to speak to her this morning. I get the feeling she's not in too much of a hurry to speak to me. I know she's seen my haircut. I'm too far away to read the expression on her face, and that's A–OK with me for now. There are more important things to consider.

'Please let the Cargavern guy be injured,' I'm mumbling to myself like a mantra. 'Please let him be injured, please please pleeeeeease.'

'Tom!' says Louise.

We're watching intently as the organisers' medical bloke

examines the Cargavern High competitor who fell over on Day One. Did he overdo it yesterday? Did he fall as hard as we hope he did? Does that pronounced limp he's got today mean they're down to a three-man team?

'Pleasepleasepleaseplease.'

I glance back to the spectators. There's no sign of Jack. I'm beginning to get a sinking feeling. I keep scanning back and forth, looking for him somewhere in the crowd.

'He's out!' yells Allan, jumping to his feet.

Louise pulls him back down.

The medical bloke is shaking his head. The Cargavern team are in an uproar. Their coach argues with the medical bloke, and the medical bloke, swiping his hand from side to side, stomps off through the snow.

Allan is very slightly pleased. 'YEEEEEEAAAH!' he roars, punching the air at waist height. 'WHAAAAYYY! Yepyepyepyep!'

His undiluted happiness is getting attention from the other competitors. Louise nudges him sharply in the ribs. 'Allan, we're not that kind of team,' she says from the corner of her mouth.

'Are now!' says Allan. 'Bam! Back in there! We can do this, guys!'

'It's still unlikely,' says Louise. 'They've got a good lead.'

'Yeh, but it wouldn't be unlikely if Freak Show would turn up!'

'That's ENOUGH!' cries Louise. 'I have had ENOUGH of your attitude towards Jack! He's got problems!'

'Too right he's got problems! He's a lazy sod who wants to get his act together,' grumbles Allan.

'Right,' says Louise. 'That's it. You and I have been out a few times, and I thought it might be tough to tell you . . . never mind what I thought, because we're not going out again. EVER. Got that?'

Allan stares at her like she's just confessed to the murder of his granny. 'What? You dumping me?' he gasps.

'If you want to call it that, yes. I'm dumping you,' says Louise.

I am very slightly pleased. 'YEEEEAAAH!' I roar, punching the air at waist height. 'WHAAAAYYY! Yepyepyepyep!'

No, I don't really. I just do all that in my head.

Allan is staring at Louise like he's just discovered she's got plans to bump off the rest of his family too. 'What? Jack your boyfriend now, is he?'

'Huh?' says Louise, eyes almost popping out of her head. 'No, he's not! I'm dumping you because you're a shallow, insensitive pig!'

'Great timing! Like it! Just as we're facing the toughest downhill of our lives!'

'Oh, grow up,' grumbles Louise to herself. 'It's only a game.'

I look over to the spectators' area again. Mum is deep in conversation with Mrs Lovelady. Mrs Lovelady has finished her soup. No Jack.

The fact that the Cargavern team is down to three people is announced by megaphone, along with the running order of the teams, which has just been drawn. Cargavern are going fourth. We're going last, which is good because it gives us a clear view of what we've got to beat.

St Something-Or-Other's-from-Poole are first off. They too seem to have had a boost in morale from the Cargavern drop-out, because their times are pretty good, all around the two-minute mark.

It's quite a long course, with a couple of turns, and the snow is smooth and compacted, very fast running. The air temperature has fluctuated over the last twenty-four hours just enough to leave a sheen across its surface. You can go like greased lightning on snow like that, if you've got the nerve.

The Cargavern Three line up one by one. Hard-nosed fury is carved into their faces. Eeek, if they're like this on a ski slope, what are they like in double French on a wet Wednesday?

The one with the haircut even more radical than mine is first up. There's a long section of this downhill course that we can't see from the area where all us competitors are corralled. He whips away from the start line, down the steep embankment ahead of us, then disappears from view until he's only three hundred metres from the end. The flags and officials at the finish are fluttering dots from up here.

The Cargavern guy spits into sight from behind a line of trees, going at a hell of a speed. He passes the post and swerves to a stop, spraying snow in a wide arc. The organiser with the megaphone who's standing by the starting line gets a message on his walkie talkie, then raises the megaphone to his face.

'One minute, forty-five point eight seconds!'

There's a round of applause from the spectators. There's a more subdued reaction from the Emerson High team. We're reckoning on one minute fifty being our average time.

Cargavern Guy Number Two: One minute, fifty-five point two seconds. Not nearly so good. Excellent!

Cargavern Guy Number Three: One minute, fifty-eight point nine seconds. Almost bad by their standards! Fantastic!

We all have to record times of less than one minute, forty-eight, to beat Cargavern on this round AND make up the shortfall from yesterday to win the competition.

We look at each other with raised eyebrows and puffed-out cheeks. Do-able. Just.

The intervening teams come and go, the starting horn sounds again and again, and nobody manages less than two minutes. I'm starting to get nervous now.

I keep turning to scan the spectators. No Jack yet.

'He probably won't be here,' says Louise, while Allan is over by the officials' table talking to the St Something-Or-Other's team. 'It's probably too soon for that.'

I let out a long, slow breath. It steams around my face, glowing in the sunshine.

'Emerson High!' calls the megaphone. 'First competitor, Allan Snyder please!'

There's a distinct feeling of tension flowing from the spectators. Voices are low and conversations are short.

All faces are aimed this way. Allan's wearing his brightest and most expensive kit which, by Allan-logic, means he's on top form and way better than the other competitors.

The horn sounds! Allan's away quickly. He's down the slope and out of sight in seconds.

We wait. Our eyes are fixed on the vertical line of the last tree on the left, dark brown against the white of the snow, the point from which he'll emerge into view.

We wait. He appears, crouched, ski sticks tucked in tightly under his arms, steady, steady.

'One minute, forty-nine point one seconds!'

Dammit. Close.

'Second competitor, Thomas Miller please!'

I'm at the start line. Breeeeeathe calmly! Ignore that violent thumping sensation, it's only your own pulse trying to club you over the head.

'Ready?' says the official with the horn-canister-thing.

'Yup,' I say.

I glance over at the spectators again. There's an extra face, behind the teachers!

Is that him?

I'm sure it's him.

I jab a quick thumbs-up. He raises a hand.

Excellent!

HHHAAANKKK!!

Go!

I kick off perfectly, concentrate on building speed. I can feel the snow beneath my skis, bumping fast. It shines up at me. Nerves are gone now. Speed and control, speed and control.

First turn coming up. Think shortest line! The snow's very slippery here. Ruts where others have passed. Easy to misjudge. I stay bent over, as close to the ground as possible, keeping a low centre of gravity.

Second turn. I must be well out of sight of the start. Stay slightly wide, too sharp and it's over. Trees away over to my right. Snow pounding beneath me, all the muscles in my legs taut. There's only the sensation of movement. Cold air skidding across my face. Out in the open, moving fast, nothing but the skis between me and a sharp smack into the ground.

The finish line's ahead of me. Stay straight! Keep on the shortest line! Arms in!

I break the invisible line of light that times the run, and rumble to a stop, slowing in a long curve. I'm out of breath, and my legs feel like they've been put through a mincing machine.

'One minute, forty-six point nine,' calls someone.

I pull my goggles over my head, and a freed dribble of sweat bumps over my cheek.

Good one.

That was a good one.

When I get back up to the competitors' area, Louise has already been called to the starting line. She gives me a salute and points to Jack. I nod wildly and take another look at him myself, as if he's something we've assembled in art class.

She's got to make one minute, forty-six or less.

The official speaks to her. She nods.

GO!

As the slicing sound of her skis moves off, I'm on my feet. Allan stands next to me, mouth agape, eyes on Louise. He's taken off his wristwatch and is holding it in front of him like a talisman.

She's already picked up speed. She's heading slightly to the right of the line I took, cutting the distance as fine as she can.

My heart's hammering again. I can see she's taking a risk, moving over to take the first turn at a very tight angle.

'C'monc'monc'monc'mon . . .'

Forty-two seconds.

She snaps out of sight.

We wait.

I take long, slow breaths. I've put my thick coat back on, but I'm shivering. I think about her, zipping down the long slope, cutting the air.

We wait.

I think about that day in France, for some reason. When we got stuck. She's got courage beyond any of us. She can do this. She can do this.

I keep watch on the last tree, not daring to blink. My eyes keep feeling iced-up. My gaze doesn't shift.

We wait.

One minute, nineteen.

We wait.

One minute, thirty.

There she is! THERE SHE IS! I let out an involuntary yelp. Move! Move! MOVE!

She's flying. She's at the line!

Allan drops back on to his seat. I suddenly realise I haven't taken a breath in about a minute and gasp loudly.

There's quiet for a moment. All the competitors are as still as statues. There's a renewed wave of murmuring from the crowd.

The official with the megaphone sniffs in the cold. He shuffles in his reflective yellow jacket.

He gets a message. The megaphone obscures his face.

'One minute, thirty-nine seconds exactly!'

ONE THIRTY-NINE! HOLY BLOODY MOLEY!

My mental commentator says it all: *The crowd go wild! It's a sensational win for the Emerson High team! They've battled the odds! They've battled each other! But more important, they've battled Cargavern High and won! Louise Wilder is THE most fabulous girl in the world, there's NO doubt about that! And Cargavern High are a big bunch of losers, so nyah-nyah-nyah! That brilliant ski-sports pundit Tom Miller, looking frankly gorgeous in his new haircut, jumps up and down as the spectators cheer!*

Louise arrives back, nose and cheeks bright red in the biting air. There's a mass mêlée of competitors and organisers and parents and teachers and shaken hands and kissed cheeks and broad grins and loud voices.

Mrs Lovelady gets to us first. 'Wilder, Miller, Snyder. Good effort,' she says, almost smiling. I don't think I've ever seen her so over-the-top excited before.

'Jolly well done!' gushes Mr Truitt, grabbing each of our hands with both of his. His four-day stubble is bristling with pride. 'Fascinating, the dynamics of an occasion like this, don't you think?'

Nope. Moving on.

Mum appears in front of me. After the obligatory hugs and well dones, she steels herself for an announcement.

Uh-oh, here it comes.

'I quite like your haircut,' she announces.

This is not the announcement I was expecting.

'But it ruins my Prince George look,' I say.

'I know,' she says.

This is not what I was expecting either. I decide to test the waters.

'I meant what I said yesterday,' I say. 'I'm packing in the Prince George business. For ever. As of now.'

'OK.'

Hmm. The waters are apparently fine. They may even have bubbles in them.

Mum steers me to one side by the shoulder. There's an odd look on her face. 'I had a good long think last night,' she says. 'I was awake until the early hours mulling things over.'

She's almost struggling to find the right words. Not

something I've seen her do before. 'What happened yesterday was, umm, something of a . . . surprise and, although I still don't quite understand what's been going on, it made me realise a few home truths. It, er, put things in perspective, it gave me more of a bird's eye view of things . . .'

'Mum, you're getting all clichéd,' I mumble.

'Yes, sorry.' She visibly composes herself and chooses her words. Good Standards do not include sloppy use of vocabulary. 'What I want to say is, while I can't altogether make sense of yesterday, it has made me reassess a lot of what I've held dear. You especially. Well, both of us, really. There are quite a few shadows that you and I have been living under for a number of years and which we need to come out from under, I think.'

The words 'my mum' and 'heart-to-heart' have never been comfortable close to each other. I'm not sure whether to feel poignantly emotive or to put my fingers in my ears and go 'lalalalalala'. One thing's for sure, though: there's been a lot of permanent change going on around here.

Mum's gaze dances back and forth around mine. 'I think, for a long time now, I've expected certain things from you. And I've not been fair. And I should respect your decisions. It occurs to me that you've put up with a lot, and that you've often kept quiet and gone along with what I wanted for the sake of a quiet life and so as not to upset me.'

Yup. Mum, you're exactly right. You're exactly right.

'Noooo,' I say.

'Anyway,' she says briskly. She swats at the air with one finger. 'I've thought long and hard. And I don't want you emulating that Prince George person any more. It's beneath you. I forbid it.'

'You forbid it?'

'Yes.'

'Er, OK.'

'I'm so proud of you, winning today.'

'So am I.'

She hugs me again. Eurgh, drippy or WHAT? But it doesn't feel like that at the time. You've got to remember, we're in the middle of a crowd of people who are all being a bit drippy. Sometimes you just can't help it.

Suddenly, Louise is right beside me and plants a kiss on my cheek. I smile at her. She's got that look on her face again, the one she had in the hotel's jaw-droppingly over-priced gift shop, the one which was very significant. Then she's gone, spirited away by Mrs Lovelady to talk to the organisers about the presentation of the trophy.

Jack is standing some way back from the crowd. He's tidied himself up, and he's huddled into his overcoat, look-ing small and alone against the widescreen vista of the snow and the trees and the sky. He's rather pale, and he's obviously dying to get away from all this. I wave and smile. He waves back.

Y'know, today just keeps getting better and better.

Chapter 14

The aeroplane going home is a big one. A BIG one. Mr Truitt is in a whole world of crap.

As we line up to board, Allan is fuming away quietly to himself. It's hard to say about what, exactly, because he's fuming away quietly to himself about so many things at the moment.

'Can't believe it,' he fumes. 'Breaking up the team.'

Ah, that's what he's fuming away quietly to himself about right now. Louise's decision to quit the team. And mine, come to think of it. And Jack's.

'Let's go out on a high,' says Louise. 'We proved we could win on our own, without Miss Annabel Norris, and we're never going to need to do that again, are we?'

'Never going to know,' fumes Allan. He glances in my direction. 'And you. Giving up on the George thing? Mad. You looked so cool with bodyguards and a posse.'

'I'm taking a leaf from Tom's book,' says Louise, all of a sudden. 'He's making a fresh start, and so am I.'

'Am I?' I say. Yes, I suppose I am.

'He's inspired me,' says Louise. 'I'm going to go full steam ahead into the world of physics from now on. It's what I really want to do. I've loved all the skiing, and I'll still do it for fun, but now it's time to move on.'

'Could have gone for a hat trick!' fumes Allan. 'Three in a row! But not any more!' He's nursing the championship trophy in his hands. I don't think he's put it down since yesterday. It's silver, shaped like a skier at full tilt, and it's about the size of an eggcup.

The queue is slowly shuffling forward through the departure gate. Mrs Lovelady is scowling at the stewardesses, Mr Truitt is handing in his completed Lost Baggage form, and Mum is complaining about the standard of airline catering. I'm pretending to be an orphan.

Louise, Allan and I are near the back of the long snake of passengers. Jack's behind us. I turn and flash him a Wallace-and-Gromit grin.

'Y'OK?' I say.

He smiles and gives a short nod. He managed to have some breakfast this morning, sitting with me and Louise in a quiet corner of the hotel's dining room.

During breakfast, he said he'd talked to Mrs Lovelady after the competition, and that she was OK. Louise grinned at me and said, 'Told ya!' The thought of Mrs Lovelady's compassionate side put me right off my scrambled egg.

I reminded Jack that he was also going to have to talk to his mum and dad at some point. He said he'd rather have his bum boiled in vinegar, but that there was no avoiding it, he guessed. And that sounded more like the real Jack.

I turn back to him again. 'Hey, Top Three Nastiest Diseases. How about: Scurvy, That-Flesh-Eating-Bug-Thing, and Having Parents?'

'Yup,' he says with a small smile. 'No contest.'

Mrs Lovelady appears and takes him aside briefly. She talks, he nods, she squeezes his hand, he nods again. Good grief, I think he's brought out her nurturing instinct again.

'Why can't YOU stay with the team?' fumes Allan.

'You heard Louise,' I say. 'I'm making a fresh start. Give it a rest, eh?'

'Look, if Freak Show won't be – OW!'

Louise gives him a sharp poke on the shoulder. 'Oi!'

'I meant HIM!' says Allan, pointing to me. 'The stupid haircut was bad enough, but – OW! Stop doing that!'

'I think he looks nice,' says Louise, sniggering.

I'm wearing a T-shirt featuring a picture of the hotel, a souvenir kilt, and a pair of long socks with thistles on them. I got them all this morning from the hotel's jaw-droppingly overpriced gift shop, and they cost me a fortune.

'Hey,' I say. 'It's part of my fresh start. Gotta start some-where!'

'Idiot,' mumbles Allan. 'As if clothes like that are going to give you a decent personality!'

'What happened to the tartan baseball cap?' says Louise.

'Well, I didn't want to look silly,' I say.

Louise laughs, her eyes folding up and her head rocking back on her swan-like neck. She looks me up and down and it starts her laughing all over again.

We're finding our seats on the plane. The low rumble of engines and air conditioning is swooshing around us, and the pooled glow from the overhead lighting is mixing reluctantly with the daylight flooding through the tiny windows.

Mum is lumbered with Mr Truitt. He's got a window seat, and is biting at his fingernails while assuring Mum that he's completely over his nerves and that the way they stick the wings on to these planes is a miracle of modern science.

Jack has got a window seat too. Mrs Lovelady is beside him, looking scarily protective. He's looking out at the runway, and I think he's glad to be going home.

'Hey,' says Allan. 'All this new start stuff. Got me thinking again. I've decided. Think those brightly coloured socks you suggested would look daft. But! On a similar line of reasoning, what about Hawaiian shirts? Fun, flamboyant.'

Louise and I look at each other for a moment. Oh! My! Gaaaaad!

'The Hawaiian look,' says Louise. 'Y'know, Tom, I think he's got it.'

'I think he's got it too,' I say. 'Darn it, that's perfect. The search is over. Hawaiian shirts it is.'

'Really?' says Allan. 'I'm thinking zappy, memorable, and as bright as my inner self.'

'Works for me,' says Louise.

'Okaaay,' says Allan. He finds his seat, whips on a pair of airline headphones and starts bopping his hands and feet to the beat. He's across the aisle from me and Louise. Oh, he's just SO cut up about Louise dumping him.

Me and Louise, sitting next to each other.

I'm not one to believe in Fate, or anything like that, but this really does seem like The Perfect Moment. She's dumped Allan, I'm in her good books, and now we'll be sitting right next to each other for almost an hour and a half.

Why not tell her how I feel? Right now!

I'm making a new start, aren't I? I'm no longer Prince George. I don't know who I am yet, not entirely, so I might as well be A Confident Guy Who Can Tell Louise How He Feels. Right?

Go on, then. Tell her. Tell her now.

Tell her how much she means to you. Tell her how much you love her. Go on.

She's got her book out of her hand luggage. It's entitled *The Evolving Universe: Six Theories That Reshaped The World* and she's about halfway through it. She's using a little bit of scrap paper as a bookmark.

I love her so much.

Tell her.

This chance may never come again. But I'm wearing a souvenir kilt.

Tell her!

She plonks the book down on her lap, and flips it shut again. 'It's no good,' she says. She leans over and kisses me, on the lips. For several seconds.

She sits back. She has that look on her face again, the one which was significant. This is why it was significant. Suddenly I understand.

'I love you,' I blurt.

Her gorgeous eyes widen. 'You . . . love me?'

Whhooaaaaaaaaoooooooaaaaaoooaoaoaoaoa . . .

'Yes,' I say, my voice weaker than a newborn kitten.

'I think you're pretty wonderful, too,' she says.

The aircraft gives a slight lurch and starts to taxi towards the runway. The sound of the engines rises and falls.

'You . . . er . . . ?'

'Do you remember that day in France? When we got lost?'

'Uh-huh.'

'You saved us both. I finally got to see the real you, the one hidden under Prince George. And the real you was the bravest, calmest, kindest person I could imagine. I think I fell for you right there and then.'

'But, I thought . . .' I burble. Hang on, think. Can't. Er. 'When you didn't . . .' What? Huh? 'I assumed you . . .'

'Prince George, I never liked. That act of yours wasn't the person I fell for, the real you. And the more you retreated into Prince George, the more I thought you couldn't possibly care about me. Besides, every other girl in the school fancied you. I didn't think I stood a chance. Heck, I only went out with Allan because I thought it'd make you jealous. Not the nicest of tactics, I know, but he'll laugh when I tell him, you know what he's like. He's pulled the same stunt on half a dozen girls before now. Anyway, it didn't work, did it!' She looks into my eyes. 'I didn't think the Prince George mask would ever drop. I'm glad I was wrong.'

The aircraft is at the end of the runway. Unintelligible pilot-talk crackles across the intercom system for a second or two.

I hold Louise's hand. 'Sorry,' I say. 'I suppose everyone's going to react very differently to me once we get home, now I'm not Prince George.'

She puts her lips very close to my ear. 'Really? So who was it they were reacting to before?'

'You're so devastatingly intelligent,' I sigh.

She laughs. The aircraft picks up speed. The engines roar, and we're pulled back slightly in our seats.

I smile to myself.

Who am I?

I'm Tom Miller.

'I shouldn't have worn this kilt,' I say. 'It's very draughty.'

She looks ahead of her, a smile playing along her lips. 'Well,' she says, 'nobody's perfect.'

Simon Cheshire hated school and, on the whole, school wasn't too keen on him either. He had a successful career in book marketing until leaving the publishing industry in 2001 to write full time.

'I was writing with the intention of getting published since I was a teenager and was turning out a steady stream of utter rubbish until I turned thirty. At that point I finally accepted that my mental age would never exceed ten, turned to children's stories and at last found my natural habitat.'

Simon has since had numerous books published. Piccadilly Press has so far published *Kissing Vanessa* and *Plastic Fantastic*.

He lives in Warwick with his wife and two children, but spends most of his time in a world of his own..

Other books by Simon Cheshire

KISSING VANESSA

Kevin is totally smitten by Vanessa, but Vanessa isn't smitten by Kevin. Everything Kevin plans to win her over seems to backfire, and his mate, Jack, who is full of wondrous tips on getting the girls somehow makes things even worse. Until one day . . .

'Hilarious and totally unpredicatable.' Publishing News

PLASTIC FANTASTIC

Fifteen-year-old Dominic is mad about the pop group, Plastic, and his interest in the lead singer borders on obsessive. He is so blinded by his devotion that he doesn't realise that his friend, Emma, is in love with him. It takes a bizarre encounter between Dominic and his pop idol to make him look at life in a totally new way.

'. . . will have you laughing so much your sides'll hurt.'
Mizz magazine

www.piccadillypress.co.uk

☆ The latest news on forthcoming books

☆ Chapter previews

☆ Author biographies

☆ Fun quizzes

☆ Reader reviews

☆ Competitions and fab prizes

☆ Book features and cool downloads

☆ And much, much more . . .

Log on and check it out!

Piccadilly Press